Drug Lord

I0655419

Alyse Zaftig

ISBN: 978-1634810630

Part 1

Engagement Party

Naelle

I stared at the coat closet in shock. There were very loud moans coming out of it.

Normally, I'd just leave them to it, but the moans sounded very familiar.

"Oh, yes, right there," someone panted.

That someone sounded an awful lot like my fiancé, the one who had put a ring on my finger just two weeks before our engagement party tonight.

Our parents were here.

Literally dozens of our friends were here, and more importantly, our parents' friends.

And Brayden was doing very loud things in a coat closet in my parents' house while our engagement party was going on.

"Naelle, are you okay, sweetheart? Where have you been?"

My dad walked up behind me and slung an arm around my shoulders.

"Why are you staring at the coat closet?"

A loud moan answered his question.

"What the..."

He yanked open the closet door, which I hadn't even thought about.

Two people came tumbling out of the closet.

"Jenny?"

She got to her feet, a little unsteady in her stilettos, her makeup an absolute mess. She had kissed off all of her lipstick...or Brayden had.

"Oh, Naelle...hi."

She ran a hand through her long blonde hair, which was a wild mess. She had clearly been in there for a while.

Brayden had gotten to his feet and was zipping his pants. He had a scrap of lace in his hand, which I realized was Jenny's tiny thong.

"Sorry about the disturbance, sir," he said respectfully to my dad.

My jaw dropped. I couldn't believe that his first instinct was to apologize to my dad — not me.

I looked at the rock on my finger. I was about to take it off and throw it at him.

But my dad beat me to the punch.

Literally.

My dad slugged my fiancé in the face, knocking him to the ground.

"Get the fuck out of my house."

"It's not a big deal," Brayden

protested. "My dad has always kept a woman on the side. It's just how families work." But he was backing away slowly, his eyes on my dad's furious face.

"It's not how my family works," my dad hissed. He looked like he was ready to pound Brayden into the ground. "Listen, I don't care about the particulars of your family's dirty laundry, but in mine, we don't cheat. And we don't cheat in coat closets with our fiancée's best friends."

Brayden held up his open palms. "I'm sorry. It won't happen again."

"You're not going to get the

opportunity to ever get in this situation again," I said, interrupting the conversation between my dad and Brayden.

I yanked off my ring, which never fit properly anyway, and tucked it into Brayden's jacket pocket.

"We're done."

"Hey, babe, we can fix this. I can fix this. I'll treat you like a princess. We can make it a real-life fairytale." He smiled at me, as if a smile could magically fix everything, as if it could erase discovering him in a closet with my best friend.

"Wait a minute, what about

me?" Jenny pouted, which was not as effective as it might have been if her lipstick weren't smeared everywhere besides her lips, as if a toddler had decided to play with her mother's lipstick and gone to town.

"And didn't you tell me that you weren't even attracted to Naelle because she's so fat?"

I gasped.

My dad crouched, gripped Brayden's arm, opened the door, and tossed him outside. Brayden didn't say anything, probably because he'd gotten a good look at my father's face.

"Brayden! Wait!" Jenny ran out

after him.

My dad closed the front door and locked it.

I loved how protective he was of me, but I said, "We still have a house full of guests, Dad."

"Right."

He unlocked the door.

"I don't think that Brayden will come back tonight, do you?"

I shook my head.

"Thanks for punching him, Dad. I know that it'll make things sticky for you."

"If I had known that he would cheat on you, I never would have encouraged you to say yes. I know that it took you two weeks to decide to accept his proposal. But I just want you to be happy, baby girl."

My jaw was on the floor. "But I've been told my whole life that I have to marry Brayden and give your company to our children. It was supposed to be the perfect corporate merger between his dad and you. We were getting married right after we graduated from college and inherited both of our trust funds."

"Fuck that asshole," my dad said. His Chicago accent came out stronger when he was completely furious. My dad was from the South Side, but he'd been a business executive in corporate America for a long time. "I thought he was a different man. I'll dissolve our partnership."

"You'd do that for me? You'd end your partnership with Mr. Wilcox?"

"I'd do that for both of us, kiddo. I don't want to be in business with someone who wants to keep a side bitch. If he lies about one big thing in his life, he's likely to lie about more things."

"Thanks, Daddy."

He gave me a hug.

"I can break the news to your mother."

"Maybe after the end of the

party?"

Both of us looked at the noisy party with live jazz and an open bar — a celebration that my parents had paid for in order to show how happy they were that I was on the right path.

I was supposed to be a 22-24-26. Married at 22. First kid at 24. Second one at 26.

And I might've gone through with it, too, if Brayden hadn't decided to cheat on me with my best friend.

"You can go upstairs, sweetheart. I know that it's been a shock. Your mom and I will take care of things down here."

"Thanks, Dad."

I looked at the door again. Brayden wasn't coming back tonight. Tomorrow, I'd have to pick up the pieces. I wasn't looking forward to telling my mother to stop planning our wedding. She was a lot happier about it than I was, and she'd be outraged tomorrow.

Running Away

Naelle

When I woke up, it was totally dark. My mother loved to stay up late, and I couldn't hear any noise coming from the party.

I looked at the glowing numbers of my clock.

Four o'clock.

There shouldn't be two four o'clocks in one day.

Yesterday came back in a rush and I wished that I hadn't woken up yet. I had to tell my mother that her vision for my future wasn't going to happen. She wouldn't have grandkids on the way in two years.

All I wanted to do was hide under my covers until the whole mess blew over.

I couldn't bear the thought of the pity from my friends and my parents' friends when they heard what went on.

And Jenny.

We were college roommates. We'd both spent a lot of time with Brayden.

I knew that she had a crush on him, but I had no idea that she would go so far as to cheat on me with him.

Her betrayal cut deeper than

Brayden's. I didn't care about Brayden very much. Even if we had gotten married, we knew that we'd leave each other alone most of the time.

But Jenny...

We'd been best friends for so long that I could barely even remember when we met in preschool.

How had I missed the signs? Everything had been going on right in front of me.

I curled up in my blanket, but I knew that my mother wouldn't let me stay there for too long.

I just needed a break from my life.

I didn't even have a job yet. I was planning on staying home and having a full-time job on the boards of several different charities.

My mom had pushed me into volunteering everywhere my whole life. I was always working on her cause du jour.

I never enjoyed any of it, except for once.

I thought about the mission trip that I'd taken in high school down to Quito to work with the Timmy Foundation at an alternative school that specialized in autistic children.

It had been one of the most

meaningful experiences of my entire life. I'd rubbed elbows not with the hoi aristoi of DC but with normal people, people who were happy with what little they had.

They lived on a few hundred dollars a month and were still happier than most of the Americans I knew.

I pulled up Google Flights to look for the next flights down there. I could either connect in Houston or Miami. It was dirt cheap, for some reason.

When I had graduated from college, I had fulfilled the terms of my trust fund. I had enough money to go anywhere in the world. I could party in Ibiza if I wanted.

But I didn't want to hang out with the spoiled rich kids who didn't have to work. I wanted to go somewhere where people were real.

So I threw a bunch of clothing into a suitcase, my guidebook to Ecuador that I bought a long time ago, and some shoes, and I was out the door before the sun rose.

Before I walked out of our tastefully decorated house, I pulled out a note.

"Gone to Ecuador. Be back later. Call me if you need me."

I smiled at how succinct the note was. I wasn't disappearing totally. The Internet in Quito was strangely faster than my Internet in DC, but at least I could get a day's worth of peace while I disappeared for just a little while.

Hostel

LATER THAT NIGHT

I rolled my suitcase down the sidewalk in La Mariscal, locally known as Gringolandia. The tourists stuck around that area, where all the bars, restaurants, and entertainment venues were.

My guidebook said that I should head for the Backpackers Inn. It looked like it was reasonably priced and centrally located.

I checked in. My Spanish was a little rusty, but it was good enough to negotiate a lower rate for prepaying for 7 days.

They finally gave me the keys — actual keys, not a key card like an American hotel would have — and I went upstairs to my private room with a window that looked out on the street. I was only a few blocks away from Plaza Foch, the center of La Mariscal.

I pulled out my laptop for the first time since I got on the plane at Reagan. I knew that my mom would be frantic, but I couldn't help it. My dad might not approve, but at least he'd understand why I'd disappeared. He probably told Mom about it this morning, before they'd discovered that I left.

As I expected, my inbox was full because my mom had completely flipped out.

I sighed and turned on my phone. I had Project Fi, so my phone worked wherever it was in the world.

It buzzed as it registered my mother's frantic texts.

I texted her back, "I'm fine, Mom."

It would be enough for the moment.

At the bottom of my inbox, I saw an email that wasn't from my mom. The subject line said *(no subject)*.

It was from Jenny.

I opened it, ready to read whatever she had to say for herself. How would she justify what she'd done to me?

All it said was: "I'm sorry."

I archived it. It would take me a while to get over her betrayal.

If she wanted him, she could've just told me. I thought that we were close.

Apparently not.

I swallowed my tears. I needed a drink.

I closed my laptop and opened my guidebook. There was a pub not too far from me that was called Finn McCool's. It was supposed to have a trivia night on Tuesdays.

All I'd had all day was some peanuts, pretzels, and Gatorade. My stomach reminded me that I needed to eat something more substantial.

It was a pub, so maybe I could find something to eat there.

Finn

Naelle

As soon as I walked inside of Finn McCool's, I realized that it was packed wall to wall. There were way too many people in a very small space.

In the US, it would probably violate the fire code to have so many people crammed together.

Did they even have fire marshals here?

I had no idea where I could sit. I looked around, totally lost.

"Hey," a guy said. "Are you looking for a team?"

I was startled to hear someone talking to me in English.

"Yeah." I realized that everyone in this section had pieces of paper in front of them.

"Welcome to the Fruitbats." He motioned to the table.

I didn't ask about the name, but I pulled up a chair at the edge.

"How do you even order here?" I looked around, but I didn't see anybody with a menu.

"Oye," one of them shouted at one of the waitstaff. "Menu!" He gestured at me.

The waiter gave him a nod and went off, a tray of discarded glasses in his hand.

A half minute later, the waiter came back with a menu.

"What do you want?"

I looked at him. He was American and probably working his way through South America.

"Could I have a burger?"

"Sure."

He plucked the menu out of my hands. I blinked as I watched him walk away. I knew that the service industry outside of America was different, but wow. He barely stopped to take my order. I'd just ordered the first thing that I saw on the menu. I guessed that they got a lot of homesick Americans here.

"What's your name?"

"Naelle," I told the guy who had flagged down the waiter.

"Pretty name for a pretty girl. I'm Emilio," he said, extending his hand. "It's nice to meet you."

It was hard to see very much in the dim light of the bar, but he looked like he had killer cheekbones and a sculpted jaw.

"Have you ever played trivia here before, Naelle?"

"No."

"Here are the stakes: if we win, we get a $100 bar credit."

"So...we want to win?"

"If we win, we'll get a jirafa."

"A giraffe?"

There were a lot of good-natured chuckles around the table.

"No," Emilio said, amusement clear in his voice. "It's a name for a very large container of beer."

"Can't you just call it a pitcher?"

"It's a lot bigger than that."

"So...what's at stake is just getting blackout drunk?"

"That's why the team is so big. The bigger, the better." He winked at me.

I took a good look around the table. We had the largest table in the whole place. It was actually the fewest tables pushed together.

"We have the biggest team

here."

"That's why we always win." He gave me a killer grin, the pure whiteness of his teeth catching the dim light of the bar.

I blushed. He looked like a charming pirate, the kind that could convince young lasses to run away with them in some kind of historical romance. I'd be his stolen treasure any day.

I blushed even harder when I realized that I was a little bit wet between my thighs, thinking about the little bit of scruff on his cheeks rubbing against the soft skin of my inner thighs.

So inappropriate! I'd barely met

this guy. I had only just broken up with my fiancé, the man whom I had believed would be my forever.

I wasn't the kind of girl who picked up men in a bar. I could count on my fingers how many times I'd even gone inside of one. I was just looking for food when I came inside of Finn McCool's.

The trivia contest started. Everyone at my table had been talking and laughing with a lot of beer bottles on the table. But when everything started, I realized why they normally won: they were ultra-focused.

Everyone talked quietly, trying not to have neighboring tables hear our answers. It was very hard when we had so many people at our table, but somehow we managed it.

Emilio was in charge of the sheet. I realized that he was somehow the leader of the group. He was dressed just like everyone else — polo shirt and slacks — but there was something about his attitude that made it seem like he should be in charge. He wore competence and cool intelligence like a shield.

He knew a lot of the answers, and when he didn't, he asked the group. We all played a fun game of Telephone.

Nearly everyone in our crew was American or Canadian, but nobody felt uncomfortable whispering in anybody else's ear. Maybe it was the alcohol. Maybe it was the late hour. But all of us were feeling pleasantly relaxed.

My burger came at some point during the competition. I pulled it as far away from the trivia answer sheet as I could.

Fortunately, they brought a set of silverware with it. I cut the burger into bite-size pieces and ate it carefully. I couldn't think of anything worse than spattering grease over our trivia answer sheet, the culmination of the whole group's work. If I messed it up, I would make a horrible first impression.

The waiter took it away pretty much the instant that I was done. Maybe the staff paid a lot more attention than I thought.

When the contest was done, Emilio brought the sheet up to be counted by the organizer.

Within 10 minutes, all the scores had been tallied.

The whole team held hands as they announced the winners.

"Third place is the Exploradoras. Second place is Wicked Wombats."

Emilio gripped my hand tightly

as we waited for the announcement of the winner.

"And with a perfect score, the winners tonight are the Fruitbats."

My whole team erupted in cheers, meanwhile I was afraid that they were going to overturn the table.

"Campeones," they chanted over and over again, sounding like a tune that I didn't know.

Everyone's hands were on each other's shoulders. The camaraderie was so sudden and utterly charming. These people had only met me tonight, yet I fit into their group instantly, as if I had known them for years.

Alley Mugging

Naelle

Two jirafas later, I was weaving a little bit when I went to the bathroom. I was grateful for the long line, since there was only one toilet for every woman in the bar. Needed its support, I leaned against the wall, not caring if it was clean or filthy.

When I was done, I made my way back to the table. I felt a little nauseous. There were still two mostly full jirafas on the table, but I couldn't take anymore.

"I'm gonna go," I slurred softly.

"Nice to meet you all."

They all waved to me while carrying on their conversations.

I walked outside. It was cold at night. I wrapped my jacket a little more closely around me.

I was barely down the block when I felt a hand grab my upper arm and haul me into an alley.

There were two of them. Both of them were armed.

"La plata!" he shouted at me. The second guy just cocked his gun. The safety was off.

Plata? Wasn't that silver? I didn't have any.

"I don't have any," I told him in Spanish.

They snorted and pointed the business ends of their guns at me.

"La plata," they insisted.

I was going to die just because I didn't carry silver.

I heard the crack of two gunshots and closed my eyes in the split second.

When I opened my eyes, I looked down at my chest, expecting to see two bullet holes.

But there wasn't anything there.

I looked at my attackers who were now flat on the ground. One of them was wearing a white shirt that had a growing bloodstain on it. It looked like a blossoming red flower that grew exponentially.

I looked behind me.

Emilio was there, kneeling next to me.

He reached for me.

"Are you okay?"

"I'm fine."

"Cut? Bruised?"

"Just a bump on the head."

"Let me see."

He touched my head gently.

"Shouldn't we turn those guys into the police? I mean they tried to mug me."

"They won't try to mug anybody else, so, no, I won't involve the police."

I looked back at the two of

them. Neither of them were moving.

"Are they dead?"

Instead of answering my question, he pulled out his phone.

"Hold still." He put his hand on my chin.

All of a sudden, a bright light was shining right in my eyes.

I tried to flinch away, but his hand held me in place.

"What are you doing?"

"Checking to see if you have a concussion. Your pupils aren't dilating properly. One of them is bigger than the other."

"It's not a big deal." I shook my head. "I've gotten minor

concussions before. I'm fine. I don't need to go to the hospital."

"You don't need to go to the hospital, but you do need to stay with someone who will wake you up every two hours."

"Why do you know so much about concussions?" I asked.

He didn't answer me.

"Come home with me."

It wasn't a question.

I tried to joke, "I wasn't expecting to go home with anybody tonight."

I earned a small smile from him. "Is there anybody else who can take care of you?"

I thought about it. I didn't even

know if the hostel owners had a first-aid kit. I doubted that they would be willing to wake me up every two hours to make sure that I was still breathing. It might be bad business if I died in their hostel.

"No."

"Then it's settled. You're coming home with me."

He pulled me into his arms.

"I can walk," I protested, even though it was really fun to be carried as if I didn't weigh anything. It was a new experience. I hadn't been carried since I was 4.

"I can carry you."

And that was the end of it. I

wrapped my arms around his neck and leaned my head against his hard shoulder as he walked further down the block.

"I'm going to let you down now."

I slid to my feet.

He took out a key fob, and then the car next to us beeped.

"Get in. Watch your head."

I opened the door and thought about getting into a car with a stranger. My mother had not raised a naive fool.

"Wait. Maybe I should just go to a hospital."

"Naelle, please. If I wanted to hurt you, I've had enough

opportunities already. You could be dead in that alley."

He was right. I knew he had a gun, but I wasn't afraid of him. He'd saved from those two thugs.

I got into his car.

First Aid

Emilio

I looked at Naelle in the backseat of my car. She didn't look like she had a concussion.

I could easily have my driver take us to a clinic. With a phone call, I could wake up a doctor and have her properly checked out.

If I really thought that she was hurt, I would do that immediately. I had a doctor on speed dial, but it wasn't necessary.

I meant what I'd said about checking on her to make sure that she didn't have a severe concussion. I could keep her up all night.

I was willing to take her home, of course, but I'd check her out first. I'd done my time in the military after going to military boarding school. I was trained as a medic, so I knew the basics, although I was a little better at tying a tourniquet than I was at caring for a concussion.

And then we were finally at my house.

"Is that your house? It's huge."

I looked at my home, trying to see it through the eyes of a stranger. I had lived here since I was a tiny child.

"It's okay, I guess."

She curled in on herself a little bit, and I frowned. I didn't want to make her uncomfortable.

I gave a nod to my driver, who took the car around the back. The garage was next to the servant's quarters.

"Come on in," I said. "I can check you out properly."

The two of us went inside of the house. I went to the medicine cabinet of the downstairs bathroom.

She sat on the toilet seat cover and waited.

"Did he touch you? Are you bruised? Any lacerations?"

"No, I don't think so. He grabbed me by my upper arms."

"Show me your arms."

She was wearing a long-sleeved shirt, and she tried to roll the sleeves up, but she couldn't roll them high enough.

"I think that I'd have to take off my shirt if you needed to see that area."

I looked at her. "I promise that I'll never touch you in a way that you don't like." I couldn't promise that I would view her as dispassionately as a health professional. My mother had pressured me towards becoming a doctor, given my rudimentary medical training, but my father had expected me to go into business, which I did.

She took off her shirt.

I stared at the angry marks on her upper arms.

"I'm going to kill them."

"No...they're long gone."

I didn't want to touch her bruises. I knew that it would hurt her, so I knelt beside her and got a very close look at them.

They were clearly hand-shaped, and it made me insanely angry to see the marks.

"Anywhere else?" I forced my voice to be normal.

But it must've been on my

face, because she backed up half an inch.

"I'm not angry at you," I said in the gentlest voice I could manage. "I want to go out there and find them."

"They just wanted silver," she said softly. "I grew up in DC. I can take care of myself."

"They wanted your wallet, and they wouldn't have hesitated to hurt you. You're not used to the rules here. It's not safe for a young woman to be alone at night."

Her back straightened a little.

"I'm capable of taking care of myself."

"Hm." I didn't say anything

else.

She didn't seem to be badly hurt.

"Let me get you one of my shirts, something sleeveless so that nothing brushes your bruises."

"Okay."

I quickly left the bathroom and ran up the stairs to grab a shirt. I took one of my softest undershirts out of its package. I should've had my housekeeper unpack it when I ordered it, but I'd been too lazy.

I brought down the undershirt to her and she put it on. What fit my torso was very long on her. She was much smaller than I was. She looked very good in my clothing.

"Do you feel okay?"

She nodded.

"Just tired."

"You can come upstairs and stay in my guest bedroom. I can check on you every hour."

"Sounds good."

She yawned.

We walked up the stairs, and I couldn't stop myself from checking out the slow sway of her hips as she went up them.

I mentally kicked myself for checking her out. She was hurt. I should be focusing on making sure that she didn't have a real concussion.

I opened the door to the guest

room that was closest to mine.

"I'll come by and check on you, okay? I'll set a timer to wake me up every few hours."

She yawned and leaned against the wall.

"Sure."

She walked slowly into her room and closed the door.

I went to my own bedroom and changed into more comfortable clothing. I set an alarm on my phone to wake me up in two hours.

First Morning

Naelle

I rolled over, my mouth dry and my head pounding. A combination of being woken up frequently during the night and a small hangover made for a pretty bad morning.

I sniffed. Was that bacon?

Before I could even get out of bed, I heard the clatter of a plate on a tray.

There was a knock on my door.

"Are you up?

I looked at myself in the mirror and almost screamed at how awful my hair looked. I was still wearing his sleeveless shirt.

"No!" I yelped. I needed to fix my hair.

"I have bacon."

"Come in."

It was okay if he had bacon. A good amount of bacon grease could go a long way the morning after.

I smelled the fresh coffee.

"You are a god."

He grinned at me, and my heart skipped a beat when he did. He was extremely gorgeous when he smiled, and I just couldn't resist smiling back at him.

I looked down at the tray and said, "There's no way that I can eat all of this."

"Of course not. Half is for me."

Half of the mountain of food on the plate was much larger than what I could manage to eat. He had an enormous fluffy omelette for each of us, and there were two bananas on the tray alongside the coffee.

I snagged a piece of bacon and took a bite.

The bacon was perfectly cooked. It was crisp with that slight hint of chewiness which was hard to achieve.

"This is perfect."

He sat on my bed and unrolled the napkins to get out silverware.

Then we ate there, as if it weren't the first morning that I'd ever eaten breakfast with him and it were completely natural for him to sit on my bed.

I'd stayed in his home despite not knowing him at all.

And he'd been a gentleman about it. I caught his eyes resting on me once in a while, but he hadn't made any moves. He'd woken me up a lot during the night, but it had been professional, almost dispassionate. I grew to hate the flashlight that he kept with him, but we knew now that I didn't have a bad concussion.

I must've been hungrier than I

thought, because the omelette and bacon disappeared in record time. I felt a little guilty, because I was sure that I'd stolen his portion of it.

He didn't seem to mind. Before I finished, he ate all of the bananas.

I sat back when I was done and touched my stomach. He put the tray on the nightstand.

"If I ate like that every meal, I'd be the size of a whale."

He shook his head.

"You are the perfect size. You have the curvy shape that I love."

There was a beat of silence between us. He was sitting right there, looking right at me.

I didn't have any experience with men. I'd dated Brayden only for our senior year of college. We knew what was expected from the both of us. His proposal at the end of the year wasn't a surprise; it had been planned for our whole lives.

He'd had plenty of fun in college, but I was more of a bookworm. I didn't party very much, instead I was too busy with my part-time job and a course load that was just a little bit more than what a normal person would sign up for. Jenny was my polar opposite. She had dated so many boys in college that I'd lost count. I'd driven to the doctor's clinic with her every time that she had a pregnancy scare. I knew how all of this worked in theory, but not in practice.

I was very curious, but I hadn't gotten very many chances to try anything.

Before I could freak myself out and talk myself out of it, I leaned forward and planted my lips on his for a firm, brief kiss.

After a half second of shock, his hands were in my hair and his mouth was kissing me back. He traveled a little lower.

I tilted my head back as I felt

the roughness of his beard on the bare skin of my neck.

He bit me hard. I gasped as the little burst of pain coursed through my body.

He soothed the bite with his warm tongue, then traveled down to my shoulder and bit me even harder there.

I could smell the clean scent of his hair from here.

I don't know how he got my clothing off, but I was naked, and he was, too.

His head traveled downwards, and he bit the inner curve of my right breast before moving to my left one.

He kept moving downwards, kissing his way down my stomach.

I was normally very self-conscious about the softness of my stomach, but he didn't seem to even care, which made me relax.

And then his head was making its way between my thighs. He parted them gently but with inexorable force.

Then his mouth was kissing me down there. My hips bucked of their own accord as my hands went to grip the back of his head as he licked me gently at first and then with a lot more force.

I didn't know if I was screaming, because I was past the

point of being able to hear, but my mouth was all the way open and my back was arched like a bow.

And still he kept going.

Every muscle in my body clenched as I experienced the most intense orgasm I'd ever had in my entire life. It was as if he'd taken part of my soul.

And he hadn't even taken me yet.

As I panted, trying to catch my breath, he rolled us so that I was on top of him. One hand was on the back of my neck, pushing me down onto his cock, which he must've guided into me with his other hand.

It felt incredibly hard inside of me as I slid down on it and took even more of him. I felt like I was too tight to take it. I felt something give inside of me.

And then finally I was all the way down, my head on his chest.

His hands went down to grab my butt.

Even though he was on the bottom, he controlled the rhythm, which was fast and hard. Every time that he stretched me, I felt like I was being taken to my limits and a little beyond.

Soon he was breathing hard under me. His eyes were shut. When he groaned, I felt him release inside of my body, which triggered another orgasm for me. I fluttered around him as my eyes rolled back in my head from the feeling of his warmth inside of me.

I wasn't a tiny little thing. I didn't want to crush him, so I tried to roll to the side. His hands tightened on my butt.

"Stay right there. I might want to go again."

I was shocked to feel the butterfly sensations as he hardened again, as if he hadn't just filled me up.

"How can you be ready so fast?"

"Must be you. You're magical."

He thrust into me, and I realized that he was already ready to go again. He sat up and put his big hands on my waist as his mouth lowered to mine.

His hands traveled from my shoulders, down my sides, feeling the indentation of my waist, before going downwards over the swell of my hips. And then he went back up.

The whole time, he kept me rocking on top of him. I felt like I was on a bucking bronco, but I never wanted it to stop.

But I was only human, and my body had other plans. Lightning struck. My mind nearly went black with the intensity of my pleasure as I jerked against his body.

With a roar, he spilled himself inside of me a second time.

This time, I rolled off of him before he could hold me in place.

"I need to clean up," I told him, feeling his seed running down my leg.

"I'll come with you."

Tub

Emilio

I followed her into the bathroom, all of my attention on the smooth sway of her beautiful hips. I knew that she felt tender because of the way that she was walking.

Even though it brought a smile to my face, because our time together had been very pleasurable, I resolved not to take her again tonight. She needed time to rest.

She climbed into the tub and turned on the water.

I climbed in and put bath gel on my hand.

"Come here."

She came to me through the water that was rapidly filling the tub.

She looked like a goddess to me — curvy with smooth, soft skin that still had my bite marks on it.

I pulled her into my lap, legs on either side of me, as I sat down on the ledge in the tub. I rubbed her luscious breasts with a little soap. Then I washed her neck and back with my hand.

My hand slipped under the water to wash the space between her legs.

"Oh," she sighed.

Her hips moved against my hand in a rhythm as old as time, her head coming to rest on my shoulder, her hair falling like a waterfall all around her, the ends tickling my shoulders.

Her mouth came to mine. She kissed me slowly and softly, her tongue gently exploring my mouth.

I didn't know how much time passed while we kissed, only that we were lost somewhere that clocks couldn't touch us.

Then she gently pulled my hand away from her core. I thought that she was done for now, but she settled down on the tip of my erection.

"Are you sure? I was going to let you rest. I know that you're sore."

"Very sure." She slid the rest of the way down.

She slid against me in the soapy water. Her hands were wrapped around my neck as she picked up the pace, rocking us both.

She was glowing from the inside, as if there were some kind of light inside of her. She was stunning, here in the bathroom, riding me as if she had all the time in the world.

I put my hand between her

thighs to flick her clit.

She screamed on top of me, her head thrown back as she crashed hard when the wave traveled through her body.

She clenched me with her wet velvet heat. I groaned as I felt her body milking mine, coaxing yet another orgasm from me.

As she rested against me, I had my arms wrapped around her. The two of us just lazily stayed right there in the tub.

Eventually, she took her head off of my shoulder and told me, "I'm about to fall asleep in this tub."

Her eyes were sleepy, so I

reached for a shower nozzle and cleaned both of us, rinsing the suds from our skin. I wrapped us in two towels, and then I carried her back to the bed.

After pulling the sheets up to cover both of us, I wrapped my arms around her towel-clad body.

"Sweet dreams, beautiful," I murmured to her.

Her only response was to sigh softly. I knew that she was already halfway asleep.

I closed my eyes.

Even though I didn't generally allow women to sleep with me, I loved sharing a pillow with her.

Guidebook

Naelle

When I woke up properly an hour later, the light was a little brighter.

The bed was empty.

I felt the sheets next to me. They were cold, meaning that I'd been left alone here.

"Hello?" I called out.

Nobody answered.

I got out of bed and looked at the sheets. There was just the smallest spot of blood, sort of like what happened sometimes during my periods.

I went to the bathroom and got a little bit of soap, then climbed on the bed and targeted the spot so I could put a little soap on it, hoping that it wouldn't stain. The sheets felt very smooth and soft. I hoped that I hadn't ruined them.

Early this morning had been incredible. I never imagined that my first time would be so sweet.

I thought that I'd be married to Brayden when I did it for the first time. I hadn't really looked forward to it.

He'd slept with so many women during the first three years of college that I'd thought about asking him for a little medical paperwork showing that he was clean.

And now, thinking about it, he must've kept on sleeping with women during the last year of college, too.

I felt very cold, alone in this bed. I didn't know if I regretted what had happened.

No, I decided, even though I felt like I was freezing now. I was glad that my first time had been like that. It wasn't what I'd expected, but it was much nicer than what Brayden would've done with me.

And it felt like there was a knife stuck in my windpipe when I thought about Jenny with him.

I didn't want to go back to DC for a while.

I looked around for my hastily discarded clothing. I should go back to the hostel. This morning had been very pleasant, and I was grateful that he'd taken care of me, but I was in a strange man's house.

What had I been thinking last night?

Sober Naelle couldn't understand Drunk and Hurt Naelle's logic. I could have gone to a hospital, gotten checked out, and only thought of Emilio in my dreams.

Here I was, the morning after, all on my own. Had I really expected it to go differently? He had been kind enough to feed me breakfast, which was definitely a nice touch. I needed to go now. In the light of day, all I felt was profound embarrassment.

I dressed quickly before I went downstairs and headed for the door.

Before I got there, though, there was a soft, "Excuse me?" in Spanish behind me.

I whirled around. There was a short lady who had closely cropped black hair.

"Hello," I said in Spanish,

figuring she probably didn't speak English.

"Are you..." she trailed off before beginning again. "Señor Emilio's novia?"

"I'm not his girlfriend, no," I said.

"Ah, I was mistaken. I'm sorry."

"It's nothing," I told her. I hoped that I had all of my things, because I was heading out to the hostel. I'd grab the Ecovia. I'd stay away from Finn McCool's from now on. I could only imagine the embarrassment of running into him again. I'd go to the hostel, journal about tonight, and move on.

I felt so free, freer than I had ever felt in my entire life. I didn't know why I felt so empowered, but I knew that a new door had opened for me.

Maybe I could have sex like that every night...it seemed easy enough to haunt bars and take men home. I was pretty enough, I supposed.

I snorted. One step at a time. It wasn't like having sex for the first time was going to turn me into a raging nymphomaniac.

I climbed the steps up to my room, and then went into the shower at the hostel to clean up, feeling sore in places that I didn't know that you could be sore.

I changed into fresh clothing after my shower, because I didn't want to wear yesterday's clothes.

What would I do today? I opened up my laptop to check on things.

My mother had sent me several more emails, but they were less panicky. She figuratively shook her finger at my impulsivity, but she said that she had talked to my dad about what had happened and she understood why I had gone. She said to take whatever time I needed to heal.

I sighed. I was afraid of my mother in a way that I'd never be afraid of my dad. He'd never be disappointed in me, but she frequently was very disappointed in my choices. At least she'd leave me alone about ditching Brayden.

I didn't know what I would do here, half a world away from my family. Ecuador was almost like another planet. I could still talk to them easily — call them if I wanted to — but I was far, far away from Brayden, Jenny, and the mess that I'd left at home.

I needed to find something to do while I was here.

I thought about going back to the alternative school, but I discarded the idea, I'd worked there and loved it, but it was weird to go back without a huge group. They'd probably push me out.

I wasn't going to stay in a hotel room for the whole time that I was here. I flipped open my guidebook.

What should I go see while I was in Quito?

There were a couple tourist sites that I wanted to check out. I'd already been to the famous church Iglesia de la Compañia, a Jesuit church which had a ton of gold in it.

The last time I was here, we hadn't had time to go up to the TeleferiQo, which was one of the highest points in Quito.

I opened up my laptop and checked out TripAdvisor. Apparently there were horses up there and I could eat lunch at the top of the mountain.

I went down and hailed a cab. There were more yellow cabs than normal cars. As soon as I stuck my arm out, a taxi came screeching to the curb.

TeleferiQo

Naelle

"TeleferiQo, please," I told him.

"No problem, niña."

I then went on one of the most terrifying car rides of my life.

My taxi driver had no problem cutting off other cars. There were loud honks every time that he did it, but he ignored them as if they were pleasant flute music.

I was gripping the seat in front of me and afraid to scream, in case he got distracted.

The drive through the city was harrowing, but when we finally got to the base of the mountain, I breathed a sigh of relief. I was pretty sure that the ride had taken at least 5 years off of my life.

He actually drove sensibly on the nearly deserted mountain road. We went higher and higher as I could feel myself beginning to pant.

Quito had a little bit thinner air than DC, but the TeleferiQo was even higher. I had mild asthma, so I was struggling to breathe as we got to the top. I cursed myself for forgetting to bring an inhaler to Ecuador. I'd left so hastily that I hadn't packed it.

Oh well.

When I got out, I paid the insane rate that was displayed on the taxi meter and walked into the TeleferiQo office.

There were two rates: one for locals and another for tourists. I paid the tourist rate and got a ticket to take the cable car up the mountain.

The line to go up wasn't too crowded. There were only four people in front of me. I stepped quickly into one of the slowly but steadily moving cars when I got to the front of the line.

I was by myself inside of the car. I was mildly acrophobic, but somehow dangling from this large cable car, I didn't feel scared. I liked looking down at the city, feeling as if I were in a sci-fi movie, floating above the Quito landscape. We were so far away that I might as well have been in the clouds.

It wasn't easy to breathe now, but I did finally get to the top. I got out and was out of breath when I walked around.

It was difficult for me to see very far. I really was among the clouds, which blocked my view from the very top of the TeleferiQo.

I was not going to make it around the area surrounding the TeleferiQo. I was a little disappointed, because I'd just paid for a ticket and a taxi ride all the way up here, but I was going to go back down.

Then I noticed a sign that said that they offered donkey rides.

Beside the sign, there was a short man with dark grey hair and a wool cap on his head.

I realized that it was a little chilly up here, even though the sun had been up for several hours. I wished that I had brought a jacket with me when I came here.

I looked to the side. There was a little girl who was standing behind a table full of scarves and jackets.

When I came closer, I realized

that they smelled strongly of llamas. I knew what llamas smelled like because my elementary school had had a llama farm next door. I lived in fear of windy days, when the stench blew towards us.

I had a clear choice here. Either I could freeze up here, or I could do as the Romans did.

I went to the little girl, who definitely should've been in elementary school, and I paid her a few dollars for a pretty, colorful scarf that had rainbow stripes and a green jacket that smelled so strongly of llama that I expected myself to begin to crave grass.

When I wasn't incredibly cold anymore, I walked back to the guy who was standing next to the donkey ride sign.

"I'd like to take a ride."

He looked at his watch.

"The next one leaves in 5 minutes. Let's get you a saddle."

He motioned to someone I hadn't noticed before.

There was another kid with black hair and tan skin that matched the guy who was running the donkey ride business.

He gave me a once-over, as if he were measuring me. Then he went to the fence and pulled off a saddle. He pulled a donkey over and fastened it.

"Try this," he said in heavily accented Spanish.

I looked at the donkey. It wasn't very tall, but I wasn't, either. How was I going to get on top of it?

I'd ridden horses in the United States a couple times, and there was always a mounting block. But there wasn't one here.

I looked around, as if it were hidden somewhere, but I couldn't see anything.

"Excuse me, how do I get on the horse?" I hoped that I didn't sound like a complete idiot.

But he snorted and pointed to

the fence.

I could feel my cheeks heating up. Of course you used the fence to get on top of the donkey. He acted as if it should be extremely obvious, but I'd never done that.

I brought my donkey over to the fence and clambered on top of it, hoping that I wasn't hurting it.

When I was in the saddle, I yelped as my donkey began to amble towards the feeding trough.

The donkey leaned down and began to eat, making me slide forward. I held on desperately to both the reins and the donkey's neck.

The boy was snickering as he

gently pulled the donkey up and away from the food.

The donkey snorted at him, but he did as he was told.

He brought me towards a group of people who were obviously tourists. They had cameras in their hands and were pointing at the different landscape that you'd find up here in the páramo.

I tried to focus on speaking quietly to my donkey, trying to make friends, but all my donkey did was flick his ears at me.

I didn't have to sit there for very long, though. Our guide was soon leading us out on a short ride around the páramo.

I was happy enough riding around on top of the donkey, and it was a little easier to breathe now, as my body got used to being at this altitude.

As I felt the stocky little donkey slowly and steadily walking along with the group, my heart soared. I just loved being up here in the clouds, far away from the city. I was cold, yeah, but it was great.

I felt like my worries in the United States were a bad dream. My reality was a simple life here in the Andes, smelling like a llama and riding a donkey on a mountain.

When I was done, I'd go back

down the mountain and just chill in my room after I got the smell of llama off of me.

I smiled when I thought of what my mother would say when she saw me like this. It was a good thing that I didn't bring a camera like the tourists had, because she'd faint.

The ride was over too soon. I saw that a bunch of the tourists were heading towards a building that smelled like food.

But I'd read the reviews on TripAdvisor, and I knew that I didn't want to eat anything up here.

So I went walking towards the

main building to get a cable car down.

But as I went downward, I noticed that there was a little cabin with steam or smoke coming out of its chimney.

Cabin

Naelle

I felt shy going towards the cabin, but the smell that was coming out of it was freshly roasted Ecuadorian coffee, which I could definitely use since it was so cold here. I figured that I could pay them for a cup.

I knocked on the door. Nobody answered.

I thought about walking away and just taking the cable car down, but I was really cold.

I'd never do this in the United States, but I opened the door and stuck my head in to say, "Is there anybody in here?"

Silence.

I knew that I should've backed out then, but the coffeemaker was right next to the door, and there was a stack of disposable coffee cups next to it. Surely they wouldn't be too angry if I took some.

I opened my purse and took out a $5 bill. If it was enough to pay for Starbucks in America, then it was enough to pay for coffee here.

I drank the hot coffee and closed my eyes while I drank nearly all of it. It was liquid bliss, the warmth spreading throughout my body.

"What are you doing here?"

My eyes flew open.

I turned around and saw Emilio standing there, with just a towel around his waist. His arms were crossed.

"Did you follow me here?"

I stammered, "No...what are you doing here?"

I dropped my coffee cup. Both of us looked down at it as it spilled just a little bit of coffee on the ground.

"Sorry," I said, grabbing a napkin and wiping up the spill.

"Why are you here?" he asked

me.

"I just wanted to go up the TeleferiQo...I had no idea that you were here."

"Were you hoping for a repeat?"

"No." I shook my head. "I had no idea that you were here. I should...I should go."

I tossed my coffee cup into the trashcan by the door and walked towards it. I should know better than to walk into a stranger's house. I didn't know what had possessed me.

But before I got there, Emilio put himself between the door and me.

"Excuse me," I said, walking around him.

But he stepped to the side.

"Why did you follow me here? This cabin is the most private place that I have. Nobody knows that I even own this."

"I didn't know that you owned this cabin," I protested. "And all I want to do is go home."

But he had walked towards me. His hands were holding my upper arms. He wasn't hurting me, but his grip was pretty firm.

"Let go," I breathed.

I saw a look in his eyes that terrified me. The lover who had made me come over and over again was gone. The man in front of me, even though he was only wearing a towel, was looking at me with an intensity that went beyond the crazy passion that we had experienced.

"Who sent you?"

"I don't know what you're talking about."

I tried to step around him again, but his hands were still on my arms.

"Let go."

"What's your name?"

"You know my name. I'm Naelle."

"Naelle who?"

"This is insane," I told him.

"Listen, I'm going to leave now, and both of us are going to forget that I ever met you." What a psycho.

But his hands were closing on my arms with more force, and I was starting to get really scared.

I was trying to remember what I'd been taught in the self-defense class that my father insisted I take before starting college. I couldn't really aim very well when he had a towel on, but a knee to the balls would be pretty effective, and he was within close range.

I shifted my weight, but suddenly he was lifting me a foot off the ground, my legs kicking but just flailing around in the air. I was completely at his mercy.

"I'm going to ask you again, and you're going to give me a real answer. What's your name?"

"Naelle Montero," I told him. "And you're going to let me go."

"Tell me, Naelle Montero," he said, with a slight emphasis on my last name. "What are you doing in Ecuador?"

I gulped. "Running away."

"From whom?"

"My ex-fiancé."

"Hm. Tell me about him." His tone made it seem like he doubted that I had an ex-fiancé at all.

"His name is Brayden Wilcox," I said. "We just graduated from college, and we got engaged. But I found him in a closet with my best friend at our engagement party."

"Nobody would be stupid enough to do that." He snorted. "Not to a girl as beautiful as you are. Pull the other one...it has bells on."

"I'm not joking," I said, twisting a little. "That's why I'm in Ecuador."

"Well, Naelle Montero, why don't we test that out?"

My eyes grew wide.

"What are you saying?"

"I can have some investigators look into it."

"Okay..." I didn't know what he

was getting at.

"While you stay in the cabin with me."

"What?" I gasped. "I want to go home."

"Don't worry. If you check out, you can go home. I'll send my jet."

"What are you talking about? How long is it going to take?"

"Just a few days."

"Are you serious?" I struggled in earnest this time, trying to twist out of his grip.

"Or I can take you home right now."

I stopped struggling. "You'd do that?"

"Why ask someone to do

something that I could easily do myself?"

"So you'd let me pick up my stuff from the hostel and take me back to America...just like that?"

He shrugged and grinned at me.

"Let's have an adventure."

I had no clue what was going on, but if he was going to let me go back to the hostel, I'd have a chance to run.

"Okay," I said.

He put me back on my feet.

"Let's go."

I couldn't wait to get out of this cabin. Emilio during trivia night and in his bed was wildly different from Emilio when I had interrupted him in his secret cabin.

I went to the lift. I saw that it was pretty much empty.

"Hello," he said to the operator, who obviously knew him well. I shouldn't ask for help here. I needed to wait until we got back to Quito.

We got into one of the cable cars, and I wrapped my arms around myself as I went to sit in the furthest corner of the car. I stared out the window.

It was a lot scarier to do it while I was descending. The ride up had been fun, but it felt like we were in a plane that was slow-motion crashing into Quito.

I covered my eyes with my hands.

"Are you okay?"

I looked at him, trying to focus on his face and not the scenery moving around our little cable car.

"I'm acrophobic."

"You felt comfortable walking into my cabin unannounced, but looking out the window terrifies you?"

"It does when we're so high up," I squeaked.

"You can look, you know. We're not going to crash. If you have trouble handling this, what are you like on airplanes?"

"Airplanes are different. If we fall, we'll pretty much die instantly. If we fall from here, we might survive or die in terrible pain."

He shook his head. "You're something else." He chuckled softly.

I kept my hands over my eyes during the entire ride down to Quito.

Packing at the Hostel

Emilio

We grabbed a taxi that was idling near the exit of the TeleferiQo.

"Did you enjoy yourselves?" the driver asked idly.

"Yes," Naelle said. She had her arms crossed as she stared out the window again. Apparently, now that we were on solid ground, she obviously felt a lot better. She was incredibly brazen sometimes, so it was a little shocking that she was so afraid of heights — or that someone who was acrophobic would decide to go on a ride up to the highest part of Quito.

"Where are we heading?" I asked Naelle.

"The Backpackers Inn," she told the driver.

Then we were flying down the mountain, and she was covering her eyes again.

I closed my eyes, too, but not in fear. My mind was ticking things off a list. As soon as we took her things from the hostel, we'd get on my jet and head straight for America. I kept a packed suitcase at the hangar. The crew knew to put it in the jet when I used it.

Then we'd go to the United

States, and I would check her out discreetly — as her boyfriend.

Nobody would need to know. I was sure that I could talk her into a simple arrangement: she would be free in America, I could check her out. If she was being truthful, I'd let her go, no harm done.

If she wasn't, then it would be a different story.

It didn't take long for the taxi driver to get us to The Backpackers Inn. I paid the amount that showed up on the meter and got out with her.

As I took her arm like a solicitous boyfriend, she had a look in her eyes like she wanted to bolt, but she'd agreed to come back to America with me.

It would be dangerous for me to let her go now. If she was sent by someone — the CIA, DEA, or one of my competitors — then she might have gotten what she came for when she'd slept in my bed.

I had no idea what was missing from my room, but if she'd taken anything, I would notice eventually. I might as well take control of the situation now.

We walked up the stairs. The hostel was nearly deserted — I supposed that most of the backpackers were out and about during the day. I didn't know if this hostel was a particularly safe place for her to sleep, but she wouldn't be here long.

She quickly packed her bags while I admired how efficient she was. She had enough clothing to last three months, but she had everything packed properly in less than an hour.

I walked her downstairs, holding her large suitcase in one hand and keeping the other one on her waist.

I could feel the tension in her back, but she didn't say anything or ask me to stop.

I was going to keep her close until I found out if she was sent to take me out.

Although if she were an assassin, she should've already killed me in my sleep. She was probably after some kind of information, but I wasn't a fool.

I didn't keep that at home.

As far as my household staff knew, I was a petrolero, one of the wealthy elite of Ecuador who had tons of oil money.

I flagged down a taxi and asked him to take us to UIO, the new airport.

Private Hangar in Quito

Naelle

I looked out the window at the private hangar. My parents were wealthy, but I'd always flown business class, not in a private jet.

Emilio apparently had one that he could easily call at a moment's notice.

Someone must have taken out my suitcase, because suddenly the handle was in Emilio's hand.

I frowned.

"Don't you need a suitcase? Are you just going to buy stuff there?"

"I keep a suitcase here."

"Of course."

It was normal for him to travel in his private jet. I was out of my depth here.

I cursed Past Naelle for letting him take her home. If I hadn't slept with him... if I hadn't decided to go up to the TeleferiQo... I wouldn't be stuck in this mess.

Still, I had to admit that I was the tiniest bit excited about going on a private jet for the first time. Yeah, the circumstances weren't ideal, but I'd take it.

I just wouldn't say thank you.

I fumed quietly as I walked in front of him. I looked at the steps.

They were sort of flimsy.

"Are they safe?" I asked him.

"Safe as houses," he said cheerfully, as if he weren't bundling me into a jet and making me go home to America.

I didn't know why he was so suspicious, but he was obviously overly paranoid. Who would think that an American tourist would be hunting them down at the top of a mountain? He obviously had issues.

"How long does it take?"

"Well, you live in DC, right?"

I nodded.

"We'll fly into Reagan. I can take you home. Meet your family."

I blinked at him. "Meet my family? As what, my one-night stand who turned out to be psycho?"

I imagined walking into my home with this guy in tow. My dad would kick his butt so fast that Emilio wouldn't know what hit him.

I smiled as I pictured it in my mind's eye.

"Okay, yeah, great idea."

"You'll introduce me as your boyfriend, of course."

"What!"

"I'm your boyfriend, at least for them. It's the simplest explanation."

"Nope," I said, crossing my arms. "Nuh-uh. No way."

"Don't be childish. It's the most efficient way to handle what needs to be done. I need to check out your story. When I'm done, you can just tell them that I was a passing fling or whatever you want. You can even tell them that you dumped me."

I looked him up and down. He looked immaculate and extremely gorgeous.

"My mom would kill me if I dumped you. She'd be dreaming about grandchildren dressed in custom-made suits the second that she saw you."

He shrugged.

"I'm willing to break her heart."

I didn't know if I was happy to deceive my family, but it was sort of a moot point. The second that I walked into my house with this guy, my dad could fix this. Yes, I had to run home to Daddy, but I had no idea that an impulsive decision made while possibly concussed would end up like this.

And he was so casual about the fact that my mom would be angry.

Whatever. The sooner I got out of this country and back on my own feet, the better.

"Get in the jet."

He motioned with his chin for me to go inside.

Stopped

Naelle

I went up the steps. When I got to the top, I stopped in my tracks.

"Are you okay?"

My eyes were wide as I looked around. Everything was either covered in leather or mahogany. It pretty much looked like the jets that you saw in magazines sometimes.

"Wow."

"Can I come in?"

I heard Emilio's voice behind me and I realized that I was standing in the doorway.

"Oh, yes, of course," I said, scrambling to the side.

He had my suitcase in his hand. I felt bad for making him wait for me to stare at everything while he was on the stairs carrying my big suitcase.

I went and sat down on one of the chairs. They were extremely soft and comfortable, almost like an armchair but on a plane.

Once I sank into it, I was already half asleep, and we hadn't even taken off yet.

I might not be happy about the situation, but I had to admit that I liked the idea of traveling to America in a private jet. I hadn't had to take off my shoes even once.

Speaking of shoes, I kicked mine off and I curled my legs under me. It would serve him right if my smelly socks stunk up the plane, but he didn't say a word.

He sat down in the chair next to mine, even though there were plenty of other places on the jet.

"No escape attempts on the jet," he warned me. "I'm going to keep a close eye on you. Don't sabotage the engines. Stay away from the pilots."

I snorted. "I have no idea how to sabotage an engine."

"Mm," he said, as if he didn't

believe me.

"What do you think I am? A Bond girl or something?"

He put his hand on my chin and gently pulled me to face him.

"Or something."

I giggled from the absurdity of being a dangerous woman.

"I'm about as dangerous as a fruit fly, honestly."

"If you were a trained assassin, it's not like you would tell me."

"Are you serious? Trained assassin? Just who do you think I am?"

"I guess we'll find out, Naelle Montero."

I pulled my chin away from his

hand, but he continued to watch me, his eyes dark.

Turning my head so I could look out the window, I could feel the motor running as the plane got ready to fly. All of a sudden, I could hear the screeching of wheels as a car zoomed past our jet and parked in front of it.

"What's going on?" I asked, but Emilio was already on his feet and walking towards the cockpit.

"What's going on?" He said it almost as if it were a command and not a question.

"No idea," they told him in Spanish.

I heard the radio crackle, but I

couldn't make out the words. I was too far away.

Emilio gritted out, "I'll go down there."

The door opened, and Emilio went down the steps to talk to them.

Little Bag

Emilio

I shielded my eyes from the fierce sunlight when I got to the bottom.

When I looked at the asshole coming out of the government car, I swore softly under my breath.

Son of a bitch.

"Hello, Señor," he said mockingly. "Fancy meeting you here."

"What's the problem?" I asked. I had no patience for this.

"Just a standard check of your aircraft. You filed your flight plan at the last minute. We're just making sure that there aren't any drugs on board. We wouldn't want any cocaine going to the United States, now, would we?"

I gritted my teeth.

"Be my guest." I gestured with my arm at my jet.

"You're welcome to check it out."

"Thank you," he said, as if he weren't a government official getting off on all this.

He went up the steps, and I followed him into my jet.

Naelle looked at him drowsily.

"Who's he?" she said in a voice which meant that she was half-asleep.

"Just someone who wants do a quick check of the plane."

"Mmm, okay?" Naelle said, her eyes shutting quickly.

The government asshole was crawling around the floor of my jet. I wasn't sure what he was looking for. It wasn't as if I would bring a shipment of our main product on my personal jet. It wasn't worth the risk. I paid a lot of mules and super-mules to bring things to market.

He crawled under a seat.

"What's this?"

What did he find, a bottle? I stopped myself from rolling my eyes. This "check" was a waste of time.

When he got to his feet, he had a very small baggie of white powder in his hand. There was a simple symbol on the bag, a big Greek omega.

I thought that he expected me to be more surprised, but I wasn't.

"This is a setup."

"I'm sorry, Señor, we'll have to take you and this lady into custody."

Naelle was awake now.

"What?"

"You were obviously snorting cocaine on this jet...one or both of you."

"That's preposterous," Naelle sputtered. "I've been mostly asleep the whole time. I haven't snorted anything in my entire life."

"Neither have I." But I shook my head at Naelle, and behind the official's back, I put a finger to my lips.

"But we're willing to come with you as we get this sorted out."

"Excellent."

He whipped out two pairs of handcuffs and put them on too tight.

Naelle yelped when he put the handcuffs on her.

"No! What the hell? You can't do this to me! I'm an American citizen."

"Just chill," I told her.

"What the hell is going on?"

"We're being taken in for questioning about the cocaine that they found in the jet."

"Cocaine? Are you joking? I've never even seen any! My dad would murder me with his bare hands if I ever used drugs."

He pulled her off of the plane. She didn't shut up.

I quietly went into the car after her. She never stopped protesting even as this man drove us into Quito, making the long journey from UIO into the heart of the city.

I didn't say much, just waited

for my moment.

Officer Ortiz

Naelle

My wrists hurt from the handcuffs. I'd never been handcuffed before, and I really didn't like it.

They were too tight for one thing, and the man ignored me.

I wished that I was home. Dad would've taken care of this.

I waited as we went to a building that was obviously a jail.

I started shaking.

"Don't worry," Emilio's deep voice said. "Nothing bad is going to happen to you."

If I could have crossed my arms, I would have.

"I cannot believe you got me into this situation." I knew he hadn't meant to, but I was also about to go to jail.

"Don't worry," he repeated. "All of this is a horrible misunderstanding. Once we are booked, we'll get out."

I turned to him, my eyebrows drawn together.

"What?" How did that make any sense?

"Just trust me."

I turned to look out the window. The guy who had found the baggie of cocaine in our jet was opening the door and roughly pulling me out of the car.

His hand on my arm hurt, but I got the feeling that if I tried to call Internal Audit on him, I'd only worsen my situation.

My hands were shaking a lot now, and my eyes were filling with tears. I considered myself a pretty brave person, but I wasn't equipped to handle going to jail in a foreign country. If I'd thought that there was even a possibility of getting arrested in Ecuador, I would've gone somewhere else. Hawaii sounded like a much better destination at the moment. At least I would've been on US soil.

Emilio got out of the car under his own power, and the official walked us both into the police station.

The second that we walked inside, there was a man waiting by the door.

"I'll take it from here, Aguilera," he said, taking my arm and pulling me away from the first governmental official, whose hand tightened painfully on my arm.

"I made the discovery. I get to book them!" Aguilera's face was red.

"That's enough," the other guy said in a tone that meant that it was the end of the conversation.

Aguilera finally let go of my arm and stomped off, muttering to himself.

"I'm so sorry, sir. He's new."

To my surprise, the new policeman unlocked our handcuffs.

I rubbed my wrists, which were red where the cuffs had chafed them.

"Not a problem," Emilio said smoothly. "Thank you for taking control of the situation."

"I apologize sincerely for the...oversight."

They shared a glance.

"I wonder how a baggie of Omega cocaine made its way onto my jet?"

The new policeman's eyebrows shot upwards.

"Omega cocaine?"

"Yes."

The policeman rubbed his chin. "Do you have it?"

"Aguilera does."

I looked at Emilio. There was something going on that I didn't understand.

"Why is that significant?"

Both of them looked at me like I was really slow. I just shook my head. Stuff was going on that I didn't understand at all.

"We should go. Is there any paperwork that you have to handle?"

The policeman shook his head. "Aguilera should know better than to stop you, Señor. I'm so sorry that he wasted your time. You're free to go."

My jaw dropped.

"Just like that?"

"Just like that." The policeman motioned towards the door. "Please go."

Before I could say anything else, Emilio's hand was on my arm and he was dragging me out the door.

Finally, we were outside of the police station.

"What the hell just happened?" I hissed, looking over my shoulder to see if there was anybody there.

"We're free," he said calmly, as if we hadn't just been arrested and handcuffed on his plane for cocaine possession.

"I don't understand anything that's happening."

"Look, we'll go to my home. All of your stuff is still in the plane. I don't think that it's a good idea to leave the country at the moment. Why don't you stay with me for a while?"

"I'd rather stay at the hostel. I paid for the rest of the week."

He pinched the bridge of his nose.

"Listen...you'd be a lot safer in

my house than you would be in a hostel now that you've been arrested with me."

"Safer? I don't feel safer after I was just ARRESTED!" I couldn't stop myself from shouting the last word.

"Shh," he said, putting a finger to his lips. There was a woman and a little boy who had turned around to stare at us.

I thanked my lucky stars that they looked like Ecuadorians, and I hoped that they weren't fluent in English. The woman said something in Spanish to the little boy, taking his hand and towing him away. Maybe it looked like a domestic dispute.

Emilio's hand tightened on my arm.

"Come to my house, please," he said again, but I got the feeling that it wasn't really a request.

He had all of my stuff, including my passport. Even if I tried to break away now, what would happen?

So I decided to stick with him and figure out how it would play out.

"I'll go home with you."

Not a Spy

Emilio

I let out a breath that I didn't know I was holding. I knew that she was headstrong, and she might be too stubborn to let me protect her.

If anything convinced me of her innocence, it was her bewilderment when we were arrested. If I'd set it up myself, I couldn't have hoped for a better result.

If she had been part of the CIA, she would've told them who she was when we were arrested, unless she was ordered to go in deep.

I considered the idea that she'd been sent as a spy...or she had planted the cocaine herself.

I snorted and shook my head at such a preposterous thought. If she'd been sent to Ecuador as a spy, she'd done a shoddy job of it. In the time that we'd been together, I hadn't seen her send so much as a text message. And a secret agent would have immediately gotten out of cuffs and run for it. An incarcerated CIA agent in Ecuador wouldn't be in a very good position. There had been enough trouble when WikiLeaks had publicized the US ambassador's candid critique of the president — I couldn't imagine the media blowout if Ecuador was lucky enough to catch a CIA agent spying here.

I'd put her in the government's hands myself. Nothing I'd do to her would equal what they'd do to her.

But now I was going to take her home, and I was going to get to the bottom of whomever had sent Aguilera to search my jet.

I was lucky that Ortiz was there, but I certainly paid him enough to look after my affairs. If he hadn't prevented it before it happened, it meant that it had been enacted at the last minute. I'd only filed the flight plan a little bit before we took off.

Heads were going to roll.

I looked at Naelle's beautiful profile.

There was something in her beautiful dark eyes — was it fear? anxiety — which awoke my protective instincts.

I was mostly sure that she wasn't sent to take me down, and I would protect her while I could get to the bottom of this. It could be a ploy to gain my trust, but I highly doubted it.

I hailed the closest taxi. I didn't normally use them, but we had unusual circumstances. I needed to get away from the police station before that asshole Aguilera even noticed that I was gone.

"North of La Carolina," I told him.

He easily slid into traffic like a seasoned Quito driver. I told him where to turn, and soon we were at my house.

Very Sleepy

Naelle

The impact of his home diminished as I got used to it. He paid the cab driver and stepped out, putting a possessive arm around my shoulders. I didn't know if I liked it. One, he was warm and solid. Two, he was awfully presumptuous for a guy I'd slept with just one night and who had proceeded to nearly kidnap me and force me to go back to the United States.

Too much had happened in the last day. I was dead on my feet.

"Hungry?" he asked me.

"No," I said, covering my mouth as I yawned.

"Let me take you upstairs to a bedroom, okay? You're sleepy."

I was too tired to think about anything, like getting my luggage. I'd figure it out when I woke up.

When I moved to go upstairs, I tripped on the first step of the staircase.

I found myself whisked off of my feet.

"Put me down?" I didn't sound very sure of myself.

"You're so tired that you can barely stand. Just let me take you upstairs and tuck you in."

I stared into his face. I could see clear affection and caring. It was totally at odds with the scary man who'd been borderline threatening when I'd gone into his secret cabin high in the mountains next to Quito.

But then I rested my head on his shoulder. I'd unravel the mystery of Emilio later. For now, I was mostly asleep.

I felt him push open a door and lean down to put me down on a soft bed.

"Stay with me." I tightened my arms around his body.

Where had that come from?

He lay next to me on the soft

bed, our arms around each other.

"I was really scared today," I told him softly.

"You're safe now," he reassured me. "I'll stay here until you fall asleep, okay?"

My eyes were closed as I accepted the embrace of this gentle monster.

Gentle

Emilio

I must have fallen asleep when I'd held Naelle in my arms, because the first thing that I felt when I woke up was her warm body still in my arms.

My hands trailed slowly down her back. I loved feeling her curvy figure.

As I opened my eyes, she was staring right at me, her mouth a hairsbreadth from mine.

I captured her mouth with mine, slowly sliding my tongue into her mouth, stroking her softly, and then withdrawing before doing it all over again.

She was whimpering softly as I pushed her onto her back and kissed her delicate neck.

I bit it.

She let out a small scream. I soothed the bite with my tongue, and her head turned to the side.

"I'm going to take off your clothes," I promised her. "If you want me to stop, say so now."

In response, she sat up and took off her own shirt. When she moved to take off her bra, I put my hand over hers.

"Stop," I said before kissing the top of her soft breasts.

"I'm going to do it."

I gently pulled her hand away from the front-clasp of her bra.

I unlatched it before freeing her breasts, then slid the straps down her arms, letting her bra fall off.

"You're so beautiful," I told her before sucking one dark nipple into my mouth.

I quickly unbuttoned her pants and slid them down her thick legs. I kissed my way down the center of her body and pushed her thighs apart.

And then I gently kissed her between her thighs. She gasped loudly and I pushed my tongue inside of her.

Her hips went wild. I held her in place with two hands on her hips as I drank her up.

She was yelling now, and I loved it, her body shuddering through a climax.

Then I turned her onto her stomach, her legs apart, and swiftly entered her.

"Oh!"

I pulled back and pushed right back in.

She pushed herself up on her hands and rocked back onto me, meeting me every time that I thrust into her body.

I prolonged the motion for as long as I could, but eventually I lost the battle and shoved as far inside of her as I could get before exploding.

I pulled out of her, turning her on her side, so that I could hold her in my arms as both of us recovered.

"That was incredible," she whispered softly.

"You're incredible," I told her before biting her earlobe, making her cry out...maybe in shock, maybe with pleasure.

I trailed a hand down the curves of her body. She was everything that I wanted and hadn't known I needed until I had her.

She yawned, and it was contagious. We'd just woken up, but I was pleasantly tired again.

"Go to sleep," I told her, stroking the soft skin of her back. "And then we'll go again."

Alejandro's Call
Emilio

But it never happened.
Instead, we were awoken by the
ringing phone.

I grunted and tried to turn
away from it. I didn't want to be
pulled out of bed by business
concerns. I'd rather focus on the
beautiful woman in my arms.

But the phone stopped ringing
for only a moment before it started
ringing again.

I cursed before I picked up.

"What?" I snarled.

"Cabrón," my little brother

shouted, "how dare you cut off my supply?"

I rubbed the bridge of my nose. I didn't want to deal with Alejandro right now.

Noticing Naelle awake and looking at me, I got out of bed, totally naked, and walked out of the bedroom.

"Ale," I said, "you know that you can't erase all of your problems with cocaine."

"I can try."

My younger brother was a mess.

I tried to soften my tone.

"Hey. I know that Mom and Dad's deaths were hard on you

but..."

"Thanks for reminding me, asshole," he said. "I've tried to forget every day."

I was the oldest and far more independent than my little brother. He was their little baby. Even when we'd been forced to go into the cocaine business, Ale had been sheltered from the more gory aspects of it.

And now I wondered if my father's decision was really the right one. If Ale saw what cocaine did to our buyers, the end consumers who bought it from our dealers, then maybe he wouldn't be so fond of the white powder that had recreated our family fortune.

"I cut you off because you need to face reality. Get a job, Ale. I already offered you one in our organization, but..."

"I don't need a job," he sneered. "Stop trying to be Dad."

Ugh. "Listen, Ale," I started.

"No, you listen," he snapped back. "If you won't let your dealers give me any cocaine, I can buy it anywhere I want. I still have my trust fund."

"You do what you want, Ale, but you know that whatever decisions you make will impact your daughter," I said. I couldn't stop him from going out on the street and destroying himself with the impure cocaine that made it to street level. At least when he took some of our inventory, I knew that he was getting pure cocaine. If he bought it, I couldn't guarantee that he'd be okay.

But I was done babying my younger brother. He was a father now. He'd made the same threat every time, promising to slow down and clean up a little, but he always did it for a day or two before going right back into his normal routine.

He was as thin as a rail, and if I didn't do something, he'd waste away. I knew that my dead parents must be turning over in their graves. My father could handle Ale, but he was gone now.

"Ale," I said softly. "I love you. I want to see you get better. Cocaine is fine as a recreational habit, like alcohol. But you have become a real cocadero. If you were an alcoholic, I'd be checking you into rehab."

"I don't have a problem," he shouted. "All my problems would go away if you'd just let me into your supply."

"I already set up a spot in a rehab program, Ale," I murmured. "I'd like for you to go there. I'll talk to our lawyers about cutting down your access to your trust fund. I don't think that you're competent right now."

"Fuck you," he said, hanging up on me.

Closet

Naelle

"Who was that?"

Emilio just shook his head.

"My little brother. He has no idea how to take care of himself. I'm figuring it out, though."

"You said something about rehab?"

Emilio shook his head again.

"He has some problems."

He abruptly changed the subject. "Would you like me to take you to the G Spot?"

I choked when I started giggling.

"Is that a weird Ecuadorian way to ask if I want to go again? Because I do."

"No," he said, kissing my neck and pinning me to the bed with his big body.

"Although I'm not going to say no to another round, I'm pretty hungry. While I'd like to keep you in my bedroom for a little longer, you should explore Quito while we're stuck here."

I was still.

"We're stuck?"

"There's something going on, Naelle. We're going to stay in Ecuador while we figure out what's happening with the Omegas.

They're out to get me."

"The Omegas? Who are they?"

"Rival business empire," he growled. "And they don't want me in their territory, even though it was mine first."

His face lost all of his anger and I saw the passionate lover who had rocked my world. He crawled towards me and pulled me into his lap before kissing me deeply.

I couldn't resist kissing him back. He tasted sweet like candy.

"If I don't stop now, we're going to end up in this bed all day."

"I'm okay with that." My eyes glazed over a little bit as I thought about spending a day in bed with him. Mmmm...

He smacked my butt with an open palm, enough to make me yelp but not enough to hurt.

"Get out of this bed before I change my mind."

He got out of bed while I was still in his arms, setting me on my feet inside of the closet.

I saw that someone had already brought my luggage into the closet. I knelt and opened it up. It seemed to be unharmed by the craziness.

I unpacked a dress, bra, and undies and put them on. I still felt sticky between my thighs, but I liked keeping him right there. I loved the idea that I would secretly smell like him, just a secret between the two of us.

He got dressed, too. When we were done, he put his big hands on my waist and drew me against his body.

"You're so beautiful," he said, light shining in his eyes. "Maybe it's a good thing that I get to keep you for a little while longer."

I put my hand on the back of his head and drew him a few inches downward to give him a kiss.

Suddenly his hands were on my waist, pulling me off the ground. I wrapped my legs around him and gave him a deep kiss.

He pulled me away and put me on my feet.

"We better get going," he said, his regret clear. "I'm going to take you to a restaurant and then swing by my brother's place. He called me, and he's mad."

"Sounds fine."

G Spot

Naelle

A car was waiting for us outside of Emilio's home. We got in and headed to the G Spot.

As he said, there really was a restaurant called the G Spot. It served unremarkable fare, featuring greasy and salty food, but it would make a good story later on.

When we were done, he paid for our meal.

As we left the restaurant, he took my hand in his, which felt twice the size of mine.

I didn't see his car waiting for us.

"How far away does your brother live?"

"Not very."

He let go of my hand to put his hand on my waist, bringing me close. He smelled fresh and clean. He was warm in the cool air of Quito. We walked at a leisurely pace on the sidewalk.

Then we were in front of a fancy hotel.

"He lives here?" I knew that Emilio was wealthy, but living in a hotel seemed like a strange choice.

"Why doesn't he live with you?"

Emilio pressed his lips

together. We were quiet for a few seconds.

"We don't really get along," he admitted finally.

"I can't wait to meet him."

I wondered if he looked like Emilio — the same dark hair, dark eyes, and killer cheekbones — or if he looked like their other parent.

I was about to find out.

We walked up to the door of the hotel. The doorman didn't even question Emilio's presence.

He just nodded at us and opened the door.

"He knows you?"

"I don't come here very often to see Alejandro, but I make a point to know anybody who might be important." He took in a breath as if he were about to say something else, but he didn't say anything.

Weird.

We got into a very pretty elevator with mahogany panels and gold-edged mirrors. I checked my hair. The plus side of being so high in the mountains was that the humidity didn't make my hair frizzy. It was pretty dry up here.

Ding. The elevator had arrived.

Emilio held the door as I walked out of the elevator. The carpet was thick enough to make me sink a little bit into it. This hotel was pretty nice.

Emilio went up to a door and knocked on it.

"Who's there?" His voice was higher than Emilio's.

"Open up," Emilio commanded.

"Joder," I heard him say before the door opened.

He looked like Emilio, although he was much more slender and maybe a few inches shorter.

His eyes were bloodshot. "Come to lecture me, big brother?"

He let us in.

The hotel suite was clearly trashed. Yes, the furniture and fixtures were just as nice as you'd expect in a hotel, but they were covered in dirty dishes and what looked like flour.

"I thought that they cut you off. Who sold you? Who would dare?"

"None of your people," Alejandro sneered. "I had to find another supplier."

I saw little plastic baggies with a Greek omega symbol on them. Emilio looked at what I was looking at. He picked up one of the baggies and took the white powder out, rubbing it between his fingers.

"I can't believe you," Emilio spat. "I tried to clean you up and send you to rehab..."

"And I didn't follow your orders. What a shock."

He reached for one of the baggies, poured the white powder out, and sniffed it.

"Is that...cocaine?" I'd never seen anybody do it before.

"You get a point." His brother's sarcasm washed right over me. I didn't care if I seemed dumb. I couldn't believe that he was snorting cocaine right in front of us.

I needed to get out of here. My dad's company was one of the major contractors for the DEA. My dad and his partner, Brayden's dad, hired a lot of ex-military guys to hunt down dangerous criminals, the kind who preyed on innocent people, getting them addicted to drugs until they either wasted away or were put in jail for stealing.

Suddenly, I understood why Alejandro was more slender than Emilio.

What was I doing here, in a dirty, opulent hotel room with a cocaine addict?

I looked at the door.

"Don't let us keep you, little girl."

I looked at Emilio, and he must have seen the worry and discomfort in my eyes.

"Listen, Ale, you can't keep living like this. You're a father now."

"Bitch only wanted a meal ticket. She was happy enough to ditch the baby."

"Where is she?"

"No clue."

Emilio banged his fist on the table.

"You don't know where your daughter is?"

"No, I don't know where my ex-girlfriend is. My daughter is at home."

I looked around the hotel, but there wasn't any evidence of a baby, which was good considering the fine film of cocaine everywhere.

"Not the Quito house."

"The Cotacachi one."

Something passed between the two brothers.

"She's fine," Alejandro mumbled. "Our nanny is taking care of her."

"Chabe?"

"Yes."

Emilio sighed.

"At least you can do that much."

"Great," Alejandro said with false cheer. "Now get the fuck out."

"I'll be back," Emilio said. I didn't know if it was a threat or promise. "And we'll have a real talk."

"Good luck with that,"

Alejandro said, opening another baggie and doing another line.

I clenched my jaw. I really couldn't be here. I knew that people did drugs, but I'd never been right next to someone doing them.

"Bye, Alejandro."

He ignored me.

I walked out to the hallway and leaned against the wall. I had my arms wrapped around me.

I felt cold, very cold. Their air conditioning must be set to the coldest setting, because I was shivering.

Emilio came out only a few seconds after I did, closing the

door with a quiet click.

He saw me leaning against the wall and braced his arm above my head. He brought his face close to mine.

"I'm sorry that you had to see that," he whispered a half inch from my face.

"Can we go home?"

Paler

Naelle

His lips touched mine gently. "Yes."

His arm was around me as we got back into the elevator. The mirror showed someone who was substantially paler than I'd been the first time around.

His arm kept me close. I was glad that he was anchoring me in place. As the elevator descended, he pulled me into his arms, so that my face was against his hard chest.

"You want to talk about it?"

I shook my head.

He kissed the top of my head.

"We'll talk about it later."

"You said that he had a daughter?"

"Sofia," Emilio said softly. "The best part of him."

When we walked out of the hotel, the doorman hailed a cab, which we got into quickly. Emilio told him where to go, and we were quickly on our way.

"How did he know that we needed a cab?" I asked Emilio. It was as if the doorman had ESP.

"I didn't come in my car."

"We could've parked nearby."

"People like me don't drive

themselves, here, cari."

"Cari?"

"Cariñosa," he said, stroking my arm gently. "I'm going to get you home and we're both going to forget about what happened today."

He kissed my cheek before moving to my mouth. I saw the driver looking at the two of us in the rearview mirror. I felt embarrassed, but Emilio didn't seem to want to stop, and I didn't know if I wanted to stop, either.

The car came to a stop after we kissed for what felt like forever.

The driver cleared his throat. Emilio dug into his pocket for cash.

I realized that I'd never seen him pay for anything with a card.

Strange.

My eyes were wide when I saw how much money he gave the taxi driver, but I didn't say anything. It was five times what I'd expect to pay for a taxi here in Quito.

Then we were getting out of the cab and going to the gate of Emilio's mansion.

Like the doorman at the hotel, Emilio's gatekeeper let us in without a word. Emilio nodded at him, sitting there in the gatehouse, and the gatekeeper gave us one in turn. I wondered if it was boring to keep an eye on Emilio's gate, but I realized that there were three or four guns on the wall behind the gatekeeper. I guessed that Emilio took his security extremely seriously.

He pulled me into the house and marched me straight up into the bedroom.

"Strip," he commanded.

I took the hem of my dress and took it off.

"You're...incredible."

He moved so quickly that I couldn't even react, but I was tumbling onto the bed with Emilio on top of me, his chest pressed to mine, his weight keeping me in place on the bed.

Wrapped Around

Naelle

My body was wrapped around his as we kissed and kissed. His tongue slid into my mouth expertly, flicking. His kiss felt like smooth, warm, fine wine trickling down my throat. Delicious.

He tilted my head so that he had better access, and I moaned quietly. His hand slid up, and he kneaded my ass in his big hand. I was a curvy girl, but his big hand could hold all of it with room to spare. I could feel my nipples harden to points as my body was melted by desire.

He picked me up, switched positions, and sat down on the bed, my legs still wrapped around his body. I unlocked them, and my knees were on the bed so I could have leverage. I slowly dry rode him, rubbing my core against the growing hardness in his pants.

He moaned into my mouth.

I unbuttoned his pants and his boxers. I took out his hard cock, tugging a little bit on it. I didn't have any water-based lubricant, but I didn't need any KY. I took a drop of his precome onto my hand, and I used it as I tugged on his cock as we slowly made out. The more precome came out, the easier it was for me to glide my hand over his shaft.

I changed the game when I reached for his sensitive balls, touching them on the underside where I knew he would feel it the most.

Suddenly, I was on my back again. I was still wearing my bra and panties, but he was in too much of a hurry to get them off. He pulled my scarlet lace panties to the side, and plunged all the way inside of me in one stroke.

My head thrashed from side to side. He felt so big, and my body burned as I stretched around him.

"Tight," he told me.

I pulsed around his dick, and he cried out. He plunged into me hard twice, before he pulled his dick out and breathed hard.

Arching my hips up, I tried to get his dick back. It was an irresistible move. He sank back inside of me to the hilt. I heard and felt his balls hitting my body, the wet sound of our bodies joining music to my ears.

He kissed me brutally hard on the mouth, forcing my lips open. His tongue slipped inside of my mouth, plunging in as deep as it could. I gagged a little bit on his tongue because of how deeply he was kissing me. His cock was tearing me apart, and I loved it.

I couldn't reach his ass as he plundered my depths, but I could reach his back still covered by his shirt. His back was completely covered in sweat. Our passion had heated him up.

I fitted my hands into the indents of his rib cage, and I pulled his body closer to mine.

"Closer," I demanded. "More."

He put more of his weight on his hands to either side of my face, and he went for broke. He rode me hard, plunging into me with so much force that I didn't know if I would be able to walk tomorrow.

One hand let go of the sheets and meandered down my body to my pleasure center. He touched me there, and I went off like a rocket ship.

He rolled us so that he was on his back.

"Ride me," he ordered.

I put my hands on his shoulders to stabilize myself, and my head fell back. His knees came up to support my back, and I was grateful. I didn't know if I could support myself with the force that we were fucking. Even though he was on the bottom, he powered up inside of me. He opened up places inside of my body that I didn't know even existed.

His hands were holding my hips as I rode him, encouraging me to go in a faster and faster rhythm. But one of them slipped between my round cheeks to touch me in a dark spot. I yelped, and I stopped.

"Move," he told me.

I slowly brought my hips up, and he touched my back door again, using my juices, spreading them backwards from my wet hole.

I didn't know if I liked it, but it was different. He pushed his fingertip inside of my ass. The rhythm was slower now as I adjusted to the feeling of my sphincter accepting his finger.

"I'll fuck you here," he whispered. "Someday."

It was a promise of fucking another time, another day. I loved it.

He sat up, using a hand behind him to stabilize himself. My smaller body was trapped between his torso and his thighs.

He kissed my neck, and then he bit my breasts, all while forcing me to come up and down on his hard cock.

I couldn't stop my orgasm from taking over my body. Every muscle inside of me tightened as I reached into the heavens and spun into infinity.

He lifted my body off of his, grasping me around my waist.

"I like your ass," he told me conversationally. "You know what I like even more? Seeing your ass as I fuck you."

He forced me to stand on my feet, and then he bent me over the bed. In the mirror on the wall, I could see us reflected back. Me, with my hair in a curtain around my face. Him, so big and strong behind me, about to fuck me from behind.

He pushed me down with a slow but strong hand. My hands hit the bedsheets. He touched my ass with his hard dick, still covered in our shared juices.

"I'm going to fuck you so hard."

With that, he shoved inside of my body in a hard thrust. I cried out from the force that he was using, with just a bit of pain in my voice. He held my hips in a way that would leave bruises, and he used my body for his pleasure. He pulled me back and pushed me forward in time to keep up with the tempo of his thrusts. And I could feel his thighs tightening.

His cock pulsed inside of my body, hitting my G-spot.

He grunted as he released a load of come inside of my waiting body. The feeling of his hot seed filling me up made me fall over the edge, too. I couldn't support myself anymore, and my torso hit the bed, my breasts flat against the bedsheets. I was totally out of breath. So was he.

I wanted to go again.

Lap

Emilio

All of a sudden, her legs were on either side of mine. Her arms were around my shoulders, her forehead on mine. Both of us gasped as she lowered herself onto me. I was still hard.

"So...big..." she panted.

Growing harder inside of her, I captured her mouth for one of our sizzling kisses.

I couldn't stop touching her. First a squeeze of her luscious breasts, then a trip down to her clit before gripping her hips and rocking her on top of me.

We didn't stop kissing as she rocked on top of me. I felt like I might explode from the intensity of our passion, but what a way to go.

She tore her mouth from mine and sank her teeth into my shoulder.

I turned my head and bit her neck.

I felt her gasp and flutter on me.

She screamed, and I knew that she was orgasming.

That's when I pulled her impossibly closer, closed my eyes, and thrust into her like an animal. The bed was making sounds as we slammed up and down on the mattress.

She was still screaming as I found my own satisfaction and poured myself inside of her.

As we floated downward, I lay back on the bed. She was still on top of me. She wiggled, as if she was getting off, but my hands were clamped to her backside.

"Stay there."

Her inner muscles contracted, aftershocks of her orgasm bringing me right back to life.

This time was softer, sweeter, and tenderer.

I let her control the pace totally, since I was so wiped out from the wildness of our first coupling.

Her hair was falling down around me as she supported herself on her hands and she moved onto me again and again, a slow rhythm that matched the steady beat of my heart.

But her movements eventually grew frantic. She sat up fully. Her eyes were closed tightly.

Then I felt her muscles going wild around me as she panted.

Her breasts were on display when she threw her head back and sang for me a second time.

I grunted as I released inside of her perfect body.

I pulled her down so that her head was on my chest, our bodies still connected. I gently stroked the smooth skin of her back and nibbled her shoulder.

"I think that you half-killed me that time."

"I think that's my line," I said, smiling even though she couldn't see it. "You're insatiable."

I could feel her body wiggling on top of mine as she laughed, and it made my body want to go again.

"How are you feeling?"

"Sore. Happy."

I stroked her back again as I felt her relax a little. She was sleepy. I should let her rest.

Rolling her to her side and then flipping her around, I put my arm over her waist.

"Sleep," I commanded.

I felt her yawn and then she was still, breathing deeply.

I loved having her in my bed. I wished that every day was like this.

I didn't want to leave her, but that thought spurred me into action. What I was about to do was far more impulsive than I normally was, but she'd been shocked and horrified by Alejandro's drug use. I knew, after dating all the women who would worm their way into my life for the money, power, and drugs, that she'd never ask for any of that. She had no clue what I could give her.

She only wanted me, and I wanted her.

So I had an errand to run. I left her there, sleeping in my bed, where I wanted to keep her forever.

Marriage Proposal

Naelle

When I woke up, the bed was cold.

"How do you feel?" His voice was coming from somewhere in front of me.

I stretched.

"Sore. I blame you." I hadn't opened my eyes.

"Open your eyes, cari," Emilio said gently.

I looked at him. He was sitting on the edge of the bed.

I stared at the box in his hands.

"Are you serious?"

"That's not a very flattering reaction."

When he smiled, his dimples appeared, tempting me to say yes.

What would it be like to wake up next to him every morning for the rest of my life?

Pretty great, I thought. I wanted to say yes, even though we barely knew each other. I knew that I loved him, even if he was often demanding and bossy.

But there was a snag.

"You haven't even met my family. I've met yours, but you would have to go back to America to meet them."

"No problem. We can just take my jet."

"You think that we can take off now?"

"Of course." He shook his head. "Do you think that I couldn't fix things? Are you surprised?"

I smiled back at him. "No, I'm not surprised."

I stared at the ring. "I'll say yes..."

Suddenly he was kissing me deeply, his tongue pushing into my mouth.

I pushed him back after 20 seconds.

"I wasn't done."

"Hm? Isn't yes enough?" He

went in for another kiss, but I put my hand on his chest and looked him right in the eye.

"On one condition."

He took a step back and arched an eyebrow.

"And what is that?"

"You have to come back to America to meet my family before we're really engaged."

"Will you wear the ring now?"

The ring was pretty much every fantasy that I'd ever had. The main jewel was an emerald, not a blood diamond.

"Yes."

He took the ring out of the box and put it on my finger.

Then he was sweeping me into his arms to kiss me.

We were making out for a while, our tongues twining together as if we were teenagers for whom kissing was the ultimate. When I regained awareness of my surroundings, I was naked on my back under him, my thighs on either side of his body.

"I'm so happy," he told me as he kissed his way down my body.

My thighs were on either side of his face.

I was very nervous when guys went down on me. I didn't like it. I had a soft stomach and pretty big thighs.

But he didn't seem to be turned off by any of that. His hands were pushing my thighs far apart as his tongue painted pure fire at my most intimate place.

My eyes closed. I felt like my whole body was turning into a puddle of molten gold.

"Oh..." I said.

Then his hands stopped pushing my thighs apart. I was wondering where he was going before one hand went to rub my clit while his tongue pushed inside of my entrance.

I went wild, bucking like crazy, fluttering around him. He kept rubbing me as I shook my way through an orgasm.

When I could speak again, I said, "That was the most intense orgasm I've had in my life."

"Just one of many, future Señora Emilio." He nuzzled my softness again.

"I don't think I can go again," I said. I was still out of breath and all trembly from the first orgasm.

In response, his hand began rubbing my clit. And my motor went roaring back to life.

"Are you sure? Do you want this?"

"Yes," I moaned. "I want it."

This time, he put two fingers inside of my channel, pushing me apart.

When he was inside, he crooked his fingers so that he stroked my g-spot.

I was wetter than I had ever been in my whole life. I felt like there was a spigot or something inside of me. I was sure that the sheets were wet beneath me. He pulled his fingers out.

Suddenly, he was flipping my body so that I was butt up, face down.

He arranged me so that I was on my stomach, my knees under me.

He pulled apart my opening as he guided himself inside.

I knew that I was sweating from the heat inside of me, like I was burning up with the best kind of fever.

My jaw dropped as he entered me. It wasn't our first time, but his size totally overwhelmed me. I could barely fit around him.

He began to surge slowly into me, going deep before pulling out.

I hugged the pillow in front of me. My fists were clenched, holding the sheets tight. I could barely stand the intensity.

Then his hand went around my neck. He wasn't choking me. He was pressing his thumb and forefinger on opposite sides of my throat.

Before I could even think about what he was doing, he was pulling my whole body backwards every time that he thrust.

The feeling of being pulled back onto him was enough to push me right over the edge. I was shuddering beneath him when I heard him shout.

And then he was flooding me with his seed. I loved the warmth.

When he was done, he pulled out of me and turned me on my side. He came and spooned me from behind.

His large hand slowly made its way from my waist to the juncture of my thighs.

I waited breathlessly as he went straight for my clit again. The pleasure this time was nearly painful. The small orgasm in the aftermath of our passion exhausted me totally.

I fell asleep like that, held safely by Emilio as I slipped into dreamland.

Coffee

Naelle

When I woke up, I opened my eyes to see that Emilio was fully dressed. I could smell coffee.

"Wake up, sweetheart."

I turned to look at the window. It was still dark outside.

"What? Come back to bed."

He came over and kissed me.

"As much as I would like to get tangled up with you again, you set a condition for your acceptance of my proposal. We're going to fulfill it now."

I sat up and his gaze

immediately went to my breasts. I blushed and reached for a sheet to cover up. I guessed that if we were married, I'd have to get used to be being naked around him, but I wasn't used to it at the moment.

"We're going back to America?"

"Yes. This is all of your luggage, right? You have your passport with you."

"Of course." I didn't go anywhere without it.

"Then we can get going."

"I'm sticky," I protested. "And I have to get dressed." And I should probably tame my hair, if I wanted to go out in public.

"I'll wash you," he said, his

eyes blazing. Without warning, he pulled me out of bed, one arm beneath my knees and the other under my back.

I squealed as he brought me into the bathroom. He slipped me into the tub and turned on the water. After he put a bunch of soap on a loofah, he began drawing big soapy circles on me. I wondered if he had ever washed anybody else before, because he didn't seem to be very experienced at it. He was only washing part of me.

"Be careful," I warned. "You might get wet."

He put the loofah down at the side. He took off his clothes as if they were rags and not ultra-expensive custom-made Savile Row couture.

"Not a problem," he said smugly.

He climbed into the tub and reached for me. I slid into his arms in the soapy water and kissed him lightly.

He didn't seem to be satisfied by the light brush of our lips. His hand was in my wet hair holding me in place as he ravished my mouth.

With a groan, he ripped our mouths apart.

"We don't have time for this. I promise, we'll have more time in the jet."

He bit the side of my neck savagely, and my body jerked against his as I moaned in pleasure.

He put soap on his hand and headed straight between my thighs, delving inside of me.

I screamed as he quickly stimulated me into an orgasm that I didn't expect. My back arched backward and my head tilted back as I panted hard.

While I regained sanity, he briskly rubbed the rest of my body with the loofah.

"Clean. I scheduled take-off for an hour from now."

"You realize that my hair is an absolute mess right now? Do you have any idea how long it takes to dry?"

"We'll just wrap it up. No problem."

He had all the answers. He turned on the shower attachment and rinsed both of us off.

I climbed out of the tub and wrapped myself up in one of the fluffy towels. He dried off and then tied his towel around his waist, snagging his clothes before going back into the bedroom. I dug around for the hairdryer and stared at it hopelessly. If we were taking off so soon, I didn't really have time to properly blow-dry my hair.

I did the best I could in a few minutes, then I tied it up in a simple bun. I was embarrassed to do such a sloppy job, but he was rushing me, and I still had to pack up.

I went back into the bedroom, where there was a red dress waiting on the bed with a scarf sitting next to it.

"I already packed for you. Get dressed."

I looked at the suitcases waiting next to the door.

I didn't know if I liked how bossy he was, but I supposed that he was used to being in charge. He worked very fast. I'd told him that I wanted to go home right before we...well...eventually ended up going to sleep. And here he was, with my things already packed and a jet ready to go.

I put on my dress and tied the scarf around my hair.

"Did you pack my makeup bag?"

"The silver one? Yes."

"But I need to put on makeup! I can't go out in public like this." My mother would faint if I went outside with my face bare. When I turned 12, she had given me a full makeup kit from MAC and told me never to come downstairs without makeup on again.

He quickly crossed the room and bent me backwards as he kissed me so hard that I nearly fell over.

"You look luscious," he told me. "Totally perfect. We need to get on the plane."

Then his hand was in mine and he was opening the door. Someone else must be getting our suitcases to the plane.

We walked out to his car, where his driver was idling.

"Ready, sir?" he asked in Spanish.

"Ready."

He kept his hand in mine as we drove through the empty streets of Quito. It was hushed and quiet at this hour, not the noisy mass of humanity that it normally was.

I was still half asleep when the car stopped at the private hangar of the new Quito airport.

He pulled me gently into the plane. Breakfast was waiting, and I looked out the window, unable to see any Ecuadorian officials trying to prevent us from taking off this time. I was grateful that I wouldn't be arrested and handcuffed again.

I wasn't very hungry. I reached gratefully for the steaming mug of good Ecuadorian coffee and drained it.

"Strap yourself in," he said.

I might not like taking orders normally, but it was definitely helpful when my brain was this foggy. It was too early in the morning for me to function normally. At this hour, it would be a miracle if I could brush my own teeth.

I clicked the buckle. He took my hand.

"We're ready," he called to the pilots. I could hear the murmur of a radio as they communicated with the air control tower.

Then we were taxiing on the runway. I squeezed his hand a

little. I wasn't a bad flier, but we were in a pretty little jet and I felt us tilt backwards. It was a lot more obvious when we were in a small aircraft than it would be in a commercial airliner.

"We'll be fine," he soothed. "Do you want some whiskey?"

"Is it a good idea to get drunk at this altitude?"

"Bottoms up."

He poured us each a little bit of whiskey from a bottle that was in a small, ice filled container at the side of the plane.

I drank it. It helped a little bit with my nerves.

He put a gentle hand on my

cheek and pulled me towards his shoulder.

"Sleep. By the time that you wake up, we'll be back in America."

I yawned and closed my eyes. He felt so solid. I knew that it was irrational, but I felt like he could save me somehow if anything happened to the plane. I slept on his shoulder.

Home in DC

Naelle

I was gently jolted when the airplane landed at Reagan.

I looked at Emilio, who was sleeping, his head turned in an unnatural position. He was going to have a sore neck.

"Hey," I said, shaking his shoulder.

His eyes suddenly opened and looked straight into mine. He was rigid for a moment before taking my hand and kissing my engagement ring.

"Are you happy to be home in

the United States? Would you prefer to live here or in Ecuador?"

"A little bit of A, a little bit of B."

I kissed the corner of his mouth. He had perfect lips. I traced them with the tip of my tongue before he grabbed the back of my head and slid his own tongue into my mouth.

The plane stopped moving.

"We better stop before we give the pilots a show."

He bit my ear, then he let go of me.

"Come on."

We got out of the plane. The sun was extremely bright.

"Did you order a car or are we going to take an Uber home?"

"I got a car. Well, my assistant did."

I raised my eyebrows at him.

"I didn't even notice you contacting your assistant."

"My jet is fitted with Internet access, so I just sent her a message. She took care of it."

I shook my head. It was as if fairies magically arranged his life to be completely perfect.

"It's a security concern," he said, shrugging.

"Security?"

"Just sensible security measures while outside of the

country."

I didn't understand why he had to be afraid in America, but whatever.

"I can't wait until you meet my parents. I'm sure my dad is going to be all alpha and tough, but they'll love you."

"If they're anything like you, I'll love them."

I loved the glow in his eyes.

"I'll take you home," I said. It was a vastly different experience from getting on his jet and getting ready to go back to America this time. He was my actual fiancé now, and my mother would be over the moon.

I'd ignored her emails, but she knew that I was safe. Dad wouldn't let his little girl be in real danger. I might've been on a different continent, but he always kept an eye on me. It was surprising that Emilio had been able to bundle me into a plane so quickly, but now that I thought about it, my dad could've had something to say about me getting into a private jet with someone that he hadn't had time to vet. He had no way to know where we were going, unless somehow he'd been able to access the filed flight plans. But why would he stop me from coming home with Emilio?

Overabundance of caution, I guessed. The pilot easily could've done an emergency landing somewhere else. Dad wouldn't have liked that.

I was glad to be home. Ecuador had been a strange adventure — I'd meant to stay longer, but here I was, back home again.

I was quiet as I looked out the windows at lots of cars going lots of places, all in a rush. The Ecuadorian way was so different from the American one.

The car eventually came to a stop.

"How did you know where I lived?"

Emilio just shrugged.

"My assistant took care of it."

It was a bit weird, but I let it pass.

We got out of the car. I went up to the door of my townhouse and opened my purse, searching for my keys. I normally used them on a daily basis, now they were probably at the bottom.

When the door opened, my dad was standing there. He stepped to the side to let me in.

"Hi, Daddy!" I said. Both of us walked inside.

To my horror, I saw him draw his fist back.

Meeting Naelle's Father

Emilio

Naelle's father's fist hit my face, and I twisted to the side to avoid as much force as I could.

He kept advancing as I blocked all of his strikes. He had good training, yes, but so did I.

He had the advantage here, because he wanted to hurt me and I couldn't hurt him. Everything that I did was defensive.

"How dare you show your face here?" my fiancée's father told me.

"Stop," I told him before catching his wrist and spinning

him before twisting his arm behind his back.

"Let go of him." Naelle's face was full of fury and confusion.

"Listen to me, both of you." I tightened my grip on her father's wrist.

"I didn't know who Naelle was, or more importantly who you were. I fell in love with your daughter purely by chance."

"Love," he spat as if it were a foul taste in his mouth. "You're not allowed to love my daughter."

"What are you talking about?" Naelle asked.

"You knew who she was," Naelle's father said. "You

manipulated her to get to me. You knew that I was investigating you and wanted to keep me from busting you for the drug lord that you are."

"Is that true?" Naelle said, tears in her eyes. "You're a drug lord, the kind of scum that my dad has hunted for years? You just played me?"

I looked at Naelle full in the face. "Naelle, I proposed to you because I loved you. Your ring...my promise...none of that has anything to do with your father. I didn't know until I looked into your background a little more deeply."

Her eyes were still filling with

tears, but her voice was steady as she told me, "You need to go now."

Her father took that moment to stomp on my instep. I let go of his arm and he whirled around the face me.

I opened my palms and raised my hands to show him that I was unarmed. I had a gun in my boot, of course, but I wasn't about to use it on her father.

"I'll go. Naelle, we'll talk later. I'm so sorry about this."

"Sorry," she spat like it tasted awful. She shook her head. "There's nothing to talk about," she told me. Now, her voice was beginning to shake. "Goodbye."

I looked at her eyes, which were full of unshed tears, and then I looked at her father, who looked like he was about to draw the gun in his shoulder holster. I could see the outline of it under his suit jacket.

"I'll go. Naelle, when you're ready to talk, I'll be waiting."

It was the hardest thing I'd ever done, but I walked out that door, leaving Naelle.

Devastated

Naelle

I watched as the door closed after Emilio.

"Do you know who that is?"

"Emilio," I said, my salty tears falling down my cheeks.

"Emilio Gabria!" My father paced. "You brought home Emilio Gabria!"

"I had no clue who he was," I protested. "When they found cocaine on the jet, he said that it wasn't his. And I got the impression from the police officer that the police didn't think that the

Omega cocaine was his, either."

"That's because his cartel's biggest rivals are the Omegas. If you found cocaine with their mark on it in his plane, then they're trying to get rid of him."

I blinked at my dad.

"So you weren't the one who kept me from coming back to America?"

"You better tell me the whole story, pumpkin."

He walked into our living room, which was as pristine as my mother always kept it. It felt surreal to walk into my DC life as if nothing at all had happened. I'd fallen in love like a ton of bricks, and all that it had earned me was heartbreak.

"There's not much to tell, Daddy."

"Humor me."

"Well...I went to a trivia night where I met Emilio."

I coughed, my cheeks heating up. I couldn't talk about this kind of stuff with my dad.

"Skip over the embarrassing parts."

I tucked a strand of hair behind my ear.

My dad choked.

"Are you wearing an engagement ring?"

His face was flushing.

"Yes," I said, blushing harder.

"How in… well, tell me about how you got there."

"I met him, um, skipping over this part, then I accidentally went into his secret cabin in Quito."

"Secret cabin?"

"It's near the TeleferiQo."

"Good to know."

I saw my dad turn to look at a pad of paper on the side table.

"Dad, I don't want you to hunt him down."

"Pumpkin, I may not have a choice. I've been trying to hunt down Emilio Gabria for years…and then he showed up on my doorstep with my daughter, who was wearing his ring."

I slid the ring off of my finger. At that moment, a ray of sunlight hit the emerald, making it light up.

"It's beautiful," I said, my heart heavy. I knew that I'd have to send it back.

"Okay, you accidentally went into his cabin, and then?"

"He was going to make me come back to the United States...he seemed really paranoid, thinking that I was some kind of spy."

"Reasonable," my dad said, nodding.

"Daddy!" I frowned fiercely at him. "Going to Ecuador was

completely impulsive. I didn't go there to hunt down a drug lord."

"But that's what you caught."

I glared.

"Do you want me to tell you what happened or not?"

He held his hands up.

"Okay, I won't interrupt anymore."

"But they...like I said, they didn't let us take off because of the baggie of cocaine that the police officer, Aguilera, found in the plane. Then Officer Ortiz let us go."

"He has half of the police force of Ecuador on his payroll. It's not like here, pumpkin. If you're an Ecuadorian police officer, the entirety of the country is your jurisdiction, and half of them are on his payroll. The other half are on the Omega payroll."

"You said you wouldn't interrupt!"

"Sorry." My dad pantomimed zipping his lips.

"And then we went back to his place. He didn't seem to think that I was a spy anymore. I met his brother, who is a huge cocaine addict, and I freaked out. We went home. When I woke up, he had an engagement ring."

"Just like that?"

"Just like that," I said, confirming it. "I told you, I fell in love like a ton of bricks. It was as if I couldn't imagine my life without him. I don't know, Dad. It was the strangest thing, but it felt so right."

I was still holding my ring.

"I know I have to send it back."

"Is that the whole story?"

"No." I sighed and looked out the window.

"I made our engagement conditional. I said that he had to meet my family before I really agreed to marry him, but he gave me the ring anyway."

"You're definitely sending it back. Now that he's met your family, there's no way that the two of you can get married. Hell, if I were really doing my job, I'd use your information to nab this guy."

"I don't think he knew who I was early on," I protested. "He didn't hurt me, even when he thought that I'd been sent to spy on him. Don't go after him."

My dad just shook his head.

"How about this? You go down to the DHL Store and I make some calls, okay?"

"Okay."

I went to get my purse and walked to the nearest DHL Store.

When I got there, I headed straight for the free envelopes and a piece of paper. I used one of the DHL pens, the kind that are attached to the countertop. It only took a little while for me to send it back to Ecuador. I didn't really know Emilio's address, but I did know the nearest intersection. In Ecuador, the address system wasn't as exact as the American one. Often, the best you could do was the nearest intersection, so it would have to be enough.

I nearly cried when I handed over my beautiful engagement ring. All of those dreams were gone. I felt like I had a hole in my heart, even though we'd known each other for such a short period.

Easy come, easy go.

Part 2

Ring Return

Emilio

"Package for you, sir."

I nodded in thanks before grabbing an envelope from my doorman. Most mail wasn't sent directly to me.

I opened the envelope and then dropped it like it was on fire.

It was a DHL package that contained something I didn't want at all.

Naelle's engagement ring had fallen out of the envelope. It sat there, twinkling innocently on the ground, as if there weren't a steel knife plunged into my heart at the sight of it here and now.

I sank to my knees. I stared at it. I couldn't pick it up.

I couldn't even breathe.

I'd done a lot of terrible things in my life. I had killed without a second thought. I sold drugs to people and made them addicted for life.

But hurting Naelle was easily the worst thing I had ever done.

And it was coming back to haunt me.

I noticed the edge of a piece of paper peeking out from the envelope's open flap. The envelope wasn't empty. There was a letter inside.

I didn't want to read it, but I had to.

I reached for the letter first. I unfolded it.

The words cut me more deeply than a razor blade.

I thought that this was mine, but it's not.

I dropped it as if it had scorched me.

We were done.

I clutched the center of my chest, but the pain didn't stop.

I knew in that moment that I wasn't going to passively accept her ring back. It belonged on her finger. She belonged to me, whether she believed it or not. I'd have to soothe her fears and fix whatever her father had told her about me, but I was willing to go the distance for her.

She was worth it.

Fish Creek

Naelle

TWO MONTHS LATER

I made some tea. The microwave in this tiny cabin looked like it was from 1980, but it still worked.

When I came back to the house, my dad had already arranged to send me to the safest place he could think of: a cabin owned by a buddy of his in the woods in the north part of Wisconsin, what Cheeseheads referred to as Up North.

So here I was, in a small cabin in Door County. I was apparently in a town so small that it was called Fish Creek. I could get groceries, I thought, but when I'd gotten here, the cabin was fully stocked with everything that I would need, as if I needed to be fortified for the zombie apocalypse. The longer that I stayed here, the lower chance I had of having to interact with the outside world.

The only thing I wanted to do was lick my wounds. I'd fallen in love too fast, and now I was paying the price of my stupidity.

Yesterday, I'd pan-fried some of the fish that I found in the fridge.

I'd woken up with food poisoning and thrown up in my bathroom, so I had to make tea to settle my stomach.

I wanted ginger ale, though. My mother always insisted on keeping some on hand, except whoever had stocked the cabin hadn't brought any.

I had a little rental car that I'd driven up from Milwaukee. I was so far north that I was basically in Canada, my cabin was very close to Lake Michigan, and eerily quiet, a little too much like a horror movie for a city girl to be really comfortable.

Up here, I was safely alone, but

there wasn't much to do. I spent a lot of time on Facebook, but doing Castleville quests was already getting really old.

I sighed. Maybe I should go into "town." They would probably have ginger ale there.

I rinsed out my mouth with some Crest mouthwash before getting dressed. I tied my hair into a sloppy bun, because I just didn't care. My mother would have a fit if she saw me out of the house with my hair like this, but whatever. There wasn't really anybody here whose opinion I cared about.

I drove for longer than I wanted to in order to get to the nearest store, a big Woodman's store.

When I got inside, everything was in disarray. I got the impression that the store stocked just about everything, if you could find it. Sort of like a room which magically produced everything you wanted but made what you wanted the hardest thing to find.

I hunted high and low for ginger ale, but it wasn't in the soda aisle. I walked through the liquor aisle, and I found it there, even though it was completely nonalcoholic.

I lugged a case of ginger ale — they didn't have anything smaller — to the register, where the cashier, a girl who was supermodel-tall and gorgeous was chewing gum. She had long, straight blonde hair and high cheekbones. She looked like she belonged on the cover of a magazine. I wondered what she was doing here, in the middle of nowhere.

I shrugged. I wasn't the only one who had problems. Fish Creek was an easy place to hide, so small that strangers were notable. I got the impression that everybody knew everybody else up here.

I was an odd girl out, with my dark eyes, Brazilian blowout, and brown skin. Everyone here looked like a Viking.

They'd been kind enough, though the little kids stared a lot more than I was used to in DC.

I put my case of ginger ale on the countertop.

"Just ginger ale?" the cashier asked.

I nodded.

"I threw up this morning."

"Do you want any medicine? Do you still feel sick?"

I shook my head.

"Nope. I don't feel sick at all. It was weird...just a little food poisoning, I guess."

She looked at me for a moment, as if trying to decide

something.

"No offense, but maybe you want to pick up one of our pregnancy tests? They're in the pharmacy section."

I felt the floor move under my feet.

"Pregnancy test?"

"Why not? No harm, right?"

I stared at this stranger who was suggesting something unimaginable.

Freaking out, I started counting in my head.

"Could you grab one for me?"

She took a quick look around the store. Nobody was there besides us.

"Sure thing."

She walked quickly with the instinct of a bloodhound. I felt like I'd been a blind woman rummaging through Woodman's, but she knew exactly what she was doing. Maybe she was native to Fish Creek, not a runaway like me.

Twenty seconds later, she had an EPT box in her hands.

"Here you go. If you take it and get a positive result, there are some clinics within driving distance...you can find an OBGYN."

I looked at her and couldn't process what she was saying. I knew that she was speaking

English, but I was flipping out.

"Thank you."

"You betcha."

I gave her my credit card and she rang me up. I hadn't used my credit card since I'd come up here, because I simply hadn't needed to buy anything.

I didn't even know which answer I wanted. If I had a baby...if I really...I was a mess.

"All done!"

She pushed the case of ginger ale at me with the EPT box on top. She slid the receipt across the counter, and then I signed it.

"Do you need a bag?"

I shook my head. I tucked the

EPT box into my purse.

Real Dream

Naelle

When I went home, I immediately went to the bathroom. I didn't know if it was performance anxiety or just plain anxiety, but I just couldn't do it. I put the stick on the counter and chugged two ginger ales, which tasted like ambrosia or unicorn tears...or maybe both.

A few minutes later, I was ready to take the test.

I put it back on the counter while I waited for the result, my mind a confused whirl. I didn't know what I was even hoping for.

When the time was up, I looked at it.

The result was positive. I was having a baby.

I couldn't process this, any of it. I knew that if I were responsible, I'd be making an appointment with a doctor to confirm my pregnancy and get...prenatal vitamins and some instructions or something. Was there some kind of parenting handbook?

I couldn't do it alone. I needed to tell my parents...and maybe Emilio.

But I had an emotional overload for the day. I couldn't do

anything but wash my hands, put on my pajamas, and go to sleep.

Somehow, even though it should have been impossible with how many things I had on my mind, I fell asleep.

* * *

I was having the dream that I had every night when I closed my eyes. In it, Emilio was with me.

"Come back," he told me.

"I can't," I told him. "I have to think of the baby."

Dream Emilio reacted differently every other time.

He exploded out of his chair and came close to me before putting his warm hand on my stomach.

"You're pregnant?"

"With your child, but we aren't together anymore."

Like a magic trick, he was holding my engagement ring in his hand. What a nice dream.

"We can be. Your child can have both parents if you just try to work with me."

"Do you think we can?" I asked Dream Emilio. "I mean, my father literally hunts you for a living. How could this ever work?"

"You know that I take what I want."

"Yes."

"I want you, Naelle. Come with

me. I promise that we'll find a way to be together."

I put my hand over his hand, which was still resting on the gentle curve of my stomach where our baby was growing.

I regretted the way that I had sent back the ring. At the time, I'd been so horrified that I was in love with a notorious drug lord that I couldn't imagine raising a child with him.

But my time here in the cabin had changed my mind. I knew that he would be a good father. He might not be a good man. He was a murderer, who ran an organization full of criminals.

But he treated me like a princess, and I knew from the way that he treated his family that his blood meant everything to him. He would love our child just as much as he loved the rest of his family.

And I knew that he loved me.

"We can make it work," I said, surrendering.

Dream Emilio kissed me just as hard as he had when we were leaving Quito. His hard, heavy body came on top of mine, pressing me into the bed.

His smell was intoxicating. It was the mix of masculine musk and dark spice that drove me wild.

And just like that, I realized

that I wasn't dreaming.

I pushed him away. He just rolled to my other side on the bed, his eyes on my face.

"You're real!"

"Yes, very real." He put his arm around my waist, drawing me close and wrapping himself around me. "Very real."

"Being away from you was hell." He buried his face in my shoulder.

My hand moved of its own volition to stroke his soft hair.

"I missed you." I was already so honest with him when I had thought that he was a figment of my imagination that it didn't feel like too much. In for a penny, in for a pound.

"I felt like my heart was empty," he told me. "But I meant what I said. Come back to Ecuador with me and we'll find a way for us to be together."

I desperately wanted what he was offering. With him in my bed, it was difficult to remember why we shouldn't be together. I was still half-convinced that this was a very strange dream.

"I'll come with you," I told him.

His tongue was suddenly in my mouth, my hands over my head, my wrists in his hands.

"I promise that I will try to

make you happy every day of my life," he said. "And there's a piece of jewelry that you need to wear from now until you die."

Somehow he was sliding the ring onto my ring finger. I knew that it had been in his hand earlier, but how had he kept hold of it while we were kissing?

I had no clue, but I knew that I would keep the ring this time around.

I'd hurt myself twice as much as I'd hurt him when I sent the ring back.

Going with him to Ecuador was definitely the right thing to do.

Our love would last forever, no

matter what we had to do to keep it alive.

Possessive

Naelle

"We're going back now."

"Now?" I blinked at him. "But I haven't packed. I'm in my pajamas."

"I don't care." He looked me over. "You're fine."

"I'm a total mess. You have to let me clean up."

"No. I'm not going to waste a single moment of our time. We're going back to Ecuador now."

He pulled me off of the bed, blanket and all.

"It's cold outside," he

explained. "I have to keep you and the baby safe."

"Are you going to carry me all the way to Ecuador?" His grip on my body was extremely firm.

"No. My driver will take us to the nearest airport. We're flying home."

Outside, there was a black SUV. He put me into the middle seat before climbing in after me and grabbing my hand.

Before, when we held hands, it was a sign of intimacy.

Now it felt like a mark of possession, especially when his thumb stroked my ring.

The drive was quiet. When we

got out, we were at an extremely tiny airport with a single runway.

"I didn't even know that they had an airport here."

"There are small airports everywhere."

We got out of the car and walked into the hangar.

It was a sharp contrast with the urban private hangars that we'd been in before. There were small covered planes.

"What are those?"

He wrinkled his nose. "Crop dusters."

It made sense that the airport mostly dealt with crop dusters, especially since we were in

America's dairyland.

We went up the steps into the jet. But something was different. The seats were gone.

"Where are your seats?"

"I stowed them. We're sitting on the couch."

"Couch?" Did he have a secret lounge somewhere?

When we walked to the back of the jet, I saw what he meant. There was a small sideways couch that had two seat belts there.

"Buckle up."

He let go of my hand for the first time since we'd left the cabin.

I buckled myself up. He slung an arm around my shoulders. It was as if he thought that I would disappear if he wasn't touching me.

"You can let go," I teased. "You have me on your jet. It's not like I'm going to go running off."

"I'm not taking any chances." He leaned down and nuzzled my neck. "I'd rather keep you right here with me."

I kissed the top of his head. He smelled insanely great. I made a mental note to ask what kind of shampoo he used. It made me want to jump on top of him.

"Ready," he called loudly.

The steps were pulled up. I felt embarrassed to have the crew see our intimacy on the back couch, but they must've had orders to basically ignore us, because the pilots just started taxiing down the single runway and getting us into the air.

"Can we get all the way to Ecuador in this jet?"

His arm tightened around me.

"We're going to stop for fuel in Miami."

"Okay," I said, and then I yawned. I rested my cheek on his head, which was still resting on my shoulder.

And I slept more deeply than I had since we were separated.

Miami

Naelle

I woke up when the plane touched down in Miami. I looked out the window and saw the heat haze outside.

Yawning, I covered my mouth with my hand.

"Stay here while we fill out some customs forms, okay? I have your passport."

I was a little confused. "Why do you have my passport?"

He shifted his weight between his feet. I realized that I was a rumpled, sleepy mess, while he looked perfect and immaculate.

"I grabbed it when we were getting your things out of the cabin."

"But I didn't agree until I woke up."

He had a guilty expression, as if I'd just caught him with his hand in the cookie jar.

"It's a good thing that I agreed to come along with you, isn't it?" I smiled. "I know you love me."

He kissed the top of my head. I could see the tension dissipating.

"Stay here. We'll be on our way to Ecuador soon."

I unbuckled my seatbelt and stretched. I loved the jet. It was luxurious and fun, but being stuck in one seat for several hours never would be fun. My face felt all oily and gross, and I needed to wipe it with water.

I had no idea where Emilio had gone. I knew that he had told me to stay in the plane, but I needed to use a real restroom, not the little one that was on the jet.

I walked down the steps. Emilio was still nowhere to be found. I shrugged and headed into the airport.

As soon as I stepped in the door, I saw my dad.

"Dad? What are you doing here?"

"We saw the flight plans. We knew that he had to stop for fuel somewhere, and as soon as we knew that he was heading for Miami, we knew that you would be here."

"What are you talking about? I'm going back to Ecuador with him."

"No, you're not. I was a fool to let you go there the first time. You're staying right here in the United States."

"Dad, I'm an adult. You can't stop me from leaving the United States if I want to go."

"You've been brainwashed. You don't really want to go."

"Dad, I…"

I stopped when he produced a set of handcuffs and cuffed my hands behind my back as if I were a criminal and not his daughter.

"Dad! What are you doing?"

"Keeping my daughter safe."

"Dad, unlock these cuffs right now."

"No." He pulled me towards a set of doors. "We have to hurry. He'll come back any moment."

I pulled back with all of my bodyweight, but my dad wasn't having any of it. He pulled me forward like I was 6 and didn't want to go to soccer practice because I got too dirty.

"Stop it!"

"I'm not going to let him kidnap you. We'll put you in therapy. It'll be fine."

"Dad, stop." I pulled on my cuffs.

"I'm sorry about this, sweetheart." And then he took a thick silver pen out of his pocket and jabbed me with the pointy end.

It wasn't a pen at all. It was some kind of tranquilizer, because all of a sudden I was falling into my father's arms.

I felt him dragging me through the doors that he'd indicated earlier.

Then I didn't feel anything.

Therapy Session

Naelle

TWO DAYS LATER

"Dad, for the thousandth time, I'm not brainwashed." I snorted. "As if he could!"

"Kid, if I thought that you genuinely wanted to be with that thug, I'd institutionalize you. Nobody would want to run away with Emilio. Don't you know what he's done?"

I was quiet. We'd had this same conversation over and over. We were beating a dead horse at this point.

"I knew what he's done," I told him. "And I want to be with him anyway."

"And that's why we have an appointment with a therapist."

"Fine."

I looked out the window. We were pulling into a parking lot in a nondescript set of office buildings in a part of town that I'd never been in before. I'd never gone to therapy before.

"We're here."

I got out of the car. At least my dad had removed the handcuffs before I woke up inside of a different plane.

Unlike Emilio's jet, the military jet had been sparse. It was functional, but it wasn't very pretty.

I hadn't spoken to my father the entire time that we flew back to DC. He knew how I felt about it. I knew how he felt about it. I knew that he was trying to do the best thing for me, but I also couldn't believe that my dad had forced me to come home when I'd clearly left of my own volition. Yes, he believed that I had somehow been brainwashed, but I didn't understand how he thought I'd been indoctrinated. It wasn't as if Emilio had hypnotized me or anything.

My phone and laptop were on Emilio's jet. I hoped that he didn't think that I'd just bailed on him, but I was worried that he did. He told me not to leave the plane, but how was I supposed to know that my dad was lurking and waiting to make me come home?

I closed the car door and followed my dad into the therapist's office, my arms crossed and a scowl on my face.

I felt like a sulky teenager.

My dad opened the office door for me. It was part of his code.

I just shook my head at him. He believed that women should be honored and protected. I always thought it was a good thing, but it was really a two-edged sword.

I went inside of the therapist's office.

My dad gave me a half hug.

"I'll be back in an hour to pick you up, peanut."

I was too old for him to call me peanut. He knew that I was an adult now. I still smiled. Unlike the bratty teenager I used to be, I cherished my father's affection.

Unfortunately, his paternal instincts had stolen me away from Emilio. I sighed. I'd had a knee jerk reaction, and I'd repented at leisure. I hadn't given Emilio a chance to talk to me about his real identity. Yes, he definitely should've told me that he was one of the world's most notorious drug lords, but he must have understood how I'd react.

I pushed open the door. Someone was sitting on a chair in the corner of the room.

"Hello."

I froze like a deer seeing headlights as I stared at my therapist.

"Emilio?"

Getting into the Car

Naelle

"We don't have a lot of time."

"What are you doing here?"

"I promise, we'll talk in the boat. But we have to go now."

"Boat?"

"Let's go out the back door."

I had no clue what was going on, but I followed Emilio to a door that wasn't the same that I'd come in.

I felt a little bad about ditching my dad. He really did want the best for me.

But I'd chosen Emilio. I knew

that it wasn't an easy choice, but I loved him.

He'd promised me that we'd find a way. I just needed to trust him.

Outside, there was a simple black Mercedes SUV.

"Is this what we're taking?" Emilio always had the finest things.

"It's reliable and unremarkable. Get in."

I hesitated for a half second right outside of the car.

Could I really do this? I knew that I was turning my back on everything that I was, everything that I had been before.

Emilio turned to look at me. Something inside of me melted.

Yes.

I got into the car.

Soon, we were scrupulously observing the speed limit. We didn't want to get any attention, while we went straight for the docks.

Car Loving

Emilio

I could see Naelle worrying, so I pulled her into my lap.

I put my hands in her hair and brought her mouth to mine.

She resisted a little bit, pulling back a half inch.

"Your driver can see us," she hissed.

I quickly hit a button to put up the partition as I pulled her closer.

"Now he can't," I murmured, touching our noses together.

I arranged her in my lap so that her thighs were on either side of me. I could feel her warm, soft body pressed against mine, and it was making me crazy.

"I missed you," I told her.

"I missed you, too," she whispered before she came in for a kiss.

Reconnecting after we'd been separated felt like coming home.

Later on, I had no clue how I'd gotten inside of her, but her panties were pushed aside while she rocked on top of me, and I knew in that moment that my home would be wherever this wonderful woman went.

I could feel my muscles tensing. I gritted my teeth to keep

myself from filling her too early, like a teenager.

Then I felt her clench her inner muscles and all of my control went straight out the door.

My eyes rolled back in my head at the pleasure. I pumped and pumped inside of her soft body, and I could feel her moving on top of me.

I muffled my cries by burying my face in her breasts, but I was sure that our driver knew what we were doing back there.

"I needed you. I need you," I whispered into her ear.

"I need you, too."

She was limp on top of me. I

held her in my arms and thanked whatever deity was watching that she was with me again.

Too soon, the car rolled to a stop.

"We have to go."

Potomac

Naelle

The Potomac was smelly and a gross color, but it was easily navigable.

"Put this on."

I looked at the life vest that he'd tossed at me.

I did the straps and sat on a bench in the small boat built for speed, not for comfort. It wasn't particularly pleasant, and I felt a bit nauseous.

"How long are we going to be on this boat?"

"Until we can get to the real

one. It's anchored in international waters."

"Why?"

"Because your father will have a harder time stealing you there."

I shut up.

I tried to enjoy the ride, but it was bumpy to go at the speed that we were going. I'd never had a problem with seasickness before, but the combination of being in my first trimester and the rough waves made me want to empty my stomach.

"We'll be at the real boat in half an hour. If you need to, lean over the side of the boat. I'll keep you safe."

Just like that, my nausea let up a bit.

We continued speeding along for a half hour. I was expecting my dad to zoom down on us in a helicopter, but nothing was in the sky — not even a single commercial plane.

Finally, we were pulling alongside a large boat, a yacht I'd say.

There was a metal ladder.

"Ladies first."

Even though Emilio might be checking out my butt from this angle, I also knew that he'd catch me if the boat moved and I fell. I might end up injuring both of us, but at least he'd break my fall.

I made it to the top without incident, and the driver and Emilio scrambled up behind me.

"What about the speedboat?"

"Someone else will take care of it. Our first priority is disappearing."

Emilio put his arm around me and guided me into the warm inside portion of the boat.

"You'll be safer in here."

Explanation

Emilio

I was relieved that Naelle was finally here, in international waters. We were still off the coast of the United States, but they'd have a harder time taking us in while we flew an Ecuadorian flag.

"Come into my quarters."

Naelle looked at the slender door of my bedroom. She looked doubtfully at it.

"Those are your quarters? It looks like a broom closet."

I smiled a little bit.

"You'll see."

She stepped through. I went in after her. She spun slowly.

"Like it?"

"It's like a tiny house or something. Just very pretty and compact."

"Functional," I said.

She sat on my bed and held out her arms like she wanted a hug. I sat next to her and pulled her into my lap. She didn't need to get naked right now. She needed to be reassured that she'd made the right choice.

"Tell me about your empire," she murmured, her head resting against my shoulder while I held her soft body in my arms.

It was time for me to come clean.

I cleared my throat.

"What do you want to know?"

"Everything."

"I'm a businessman, first and foremost."

She snorted.

"I am. Moving drugs is a business just like any other."

"Except that it's *illegal.*"

I shrugged. "Well, there's that."

"How did you get into it?"

"I thought that I was going to be a petrolero, which was my father's profession, and it had kept our family comfortably wealthy my entire life. I could have sat back on my millions and lived comfortably on the interest for my entire life."

"And then?"

"Then, dollarization happened. Suddenly, our money had been reduced to a shadow of what it was."

I held her a little tighter. It wasn't easy to remember the time when my entire life had fallen apart.

"We could've fallen to pieces. There were plenty of people at our level who did. They didn't know how to live or work. They didn't sully their hands with plebeian concerns, like making enough money to put food on the table."

"What saved you? What made you different from the rest?"

"We had a secret weapon: my mother. She'd been a wealthy middle-class girl when she'd met my father at PUCE, a university in Quito. My maternal grandfather had struggled as a businessman until she was a teenager, when he'd finally signed a few contracts to export roses to the United States."

"Roses?"

"Yes, roses. Valentine's Day was the biggest event of the year for them. My mother had been raised to think that she should work for a living, even though she'd gone through all the etiquette classes that a teenager should go through."

"So she's part of both worlds."

"Yes. She fit into my father's family with its bloodline that went back to the Spaniards from the colonial days, but my paternal grandparents had always been rather snide about her somewhat humble upbringing, since my maternal grandfather actually worked and continued to work, even when he had more than enough money."

She whistled softly. "Your grandfather sounds interesting."

"My mother is a strong woman.

It was my mother who thought of buying farmland in the Andes. It was my mother who had hired people to cultivate ancient plants, plants that had been grown there for millennia."

"Coca."

"Coca," I confirmed. "It was legal in Ecuador to cultivate coca. After all, it was highly important for indigenous cultural rituals. In addition, altitude sickness, what some people called sorojchi, could be cured with coca. And in the mountains, who would know?"

"So your mother was the one who got you into the cocaine business?"

"Yup. We rebuilt our fortune with kilo after kilo of white powder that our customers couldn't wait to get. And we'd kept our house, the one that was registered as a historical landmark, and our lands that UNESCO almost stole since they had pre-Columbian pyramids on them. Money talks."

Naelle was quiet.

"Thank you for sharing your perspective. Have you ever thought about the cost to society? Obviously, running drugs is lucrative, and it probably saved your family."

"It did."

"But at a high cost to other

people."

"Naelle...I'll do everything in my power to help and protect people I consider mine. Beyond that, I don't care. They aren't forced to buy my products at gunpoint. If they wanted to go to rehab and get clean, they could. You can't fight human nature."

"How many people have you killed?"

"Probably too many to count. Not personally, but there's been a high death toll."

She was quiet and still in my lap. She climbed out.

"Are you okay?"

"It's been a rough day. I think

I'll just try to brush my teeth and go to sleep."

"Of course."

Belt and Headboard

Emilio

I undressed, getting comfortable in my small bed. I accidentally thunked my head on the metal headboard. When she came out of the bathroom, she was wrapped in a towel. I impulsively got to my feet and put my arms around her, drawing her closer, smelling the sweet scent of her hair. Was it strawberry? Apple? Whatever it was, it was fucking delicious. I needed to taste her.

I threw her on the bed, then I surrounded her with my body. She was mine.

I kissed her throat delicately, and she made a noise deep in her throat, one that I didn't think that she could control.

I smiled.

I gathered her wrists in one of my hands and pinned them to the bed. She gasped and opened her eyes. My other hand slid between her legs, touching her clit, coaxing it out of its hiding place. She cried out when I amped up the pace, arching her hips into my hand, totally lost.

I looked around for something to secure her hands. I saw my belt on the floor. Perfect.

I let go of her hands, and I slid off the bed.

"Where are you going?" she demanded. "What are you doing?"

"Shh," I told her.

Her eyes widened when she saw the belt in my hand. Without a word, I bound her hands together, looping the excess length around part of the small headboard before buckling my belt.

I stopped to admire my handiwork. She looked so beautiful decorating my bed. Her body was perfect, all luscious curves, and I knew that she was all mine.

Now that she was tied up, it was time to eat her.

I spread her legs apart, so that her glistening folds were displayed for me. She had nowhere to hide.

I touched her little clit with my tongue, and I sucked, just a little.

She reacted violently, bucking her hips up towards me.

I reared back.

"Don't stop! Please don't stop! I'll do anything."

"I can't go down on you if you buck me off, sweetheart. Obviously that belt is not enough to keep you still. I want you to keep still, real still, or this is over."

"I'll be still. I promise," she whispered.

"That's my girl."

I bent back down, caressing the soft, smooth skin of her juicy thighs, and I licked her slit from the bottom to the very top. Though I knew that her reaction was just as strong as before, she was staying still like I had told her to.

Good girls get rewarded.

I brought my fingers into play, sliding one into her slit as I went back to sucking on her clit.

From the shaking of her body, I knew that she was holding back. Her breathing was hard, desperate for more.

I gave it to her.

I slid my finger to her front wall, right towards her G-spot, and she sang for me.

I had never heard anything more beautiful. Beethoven had nothing on the girl I had screaming beneath me on this bed. She was an enchantress, seducing me with her delicious body. I was going to lick it up. All of it.

Slow and Sweet

Naelle

I was breathing as if I had just run a marathon. My wrists chafed a little where I had pulled against the belt while in the throes of ecstasy. I didn't care, though. A little pleasure with my pain was just fine.

He bit me on my upper thigh, and I screamed. I wanted to move so badly, but I couldn't.

He stopped licking my pussy, and instead he kissed his way up my body.

"I have been neglecting these

beautiful breasts," he said, pinching my nipples. "I think that's something that I'm going to fix."

I watched his hair as he bit my breasts, gently nipping at first. Then, he started savagely biting me. The sensation went on a straight line down to my core, as if he were sending exploding rockets of sensation right into me.

I loved it. I wanted to arch my back up under him, but I had promised to be still. I couldn't control how hard I was breathing, though.

He shifted down my body, and he threw my legs over his shoulders.

"Enough. I love tonguing your body, but I think it's time for the main course."

I felt the hard crown of his cock touch my slit. I was wet, very wet, but he was so big.

I didn't know if he was going to fit.

"I don't..."

He interrupted me by shoving everything inside of me.

I screamed in pain and pleasure. They raced neck and neck and caught me in unbearable sensation. I couldn't keep my promise not to move anymore, though my range of motion was severely limited by this position, I pushed my hips up at him, and he pushed me back with equal force, enough force to break the bed.

His eyes stared straight into mine. There was something tender and loving in his face, though his body was taking me as roughly as possible, in a hard rhythm that would leave me sore for days.

I felt a rush of precome spill inside of me, and my body was warmed from the inside out. He stretched my legs as he pushed harder and deeper inside of me, parting my slick folds. The scent of sex was everywhere.

He went for it in earnest now. Instead of a hard rhythm, he

switched to animalistic, irregular thrusts. I knew he was getting close.

His hand went between my legs to find my clit. He rubbed it, and I couldn't help it. An explosion of white fire filled my brain, and I panted as my body fluttered and contracted around him.

He moved so that he was flat on me, my toes touching the bed. He slammed into me with as much force as he could muster. The slap of skin filled my ears and turned me on, though I'd already had my orgasm.

He stopped and withdrew from me.

Before I could react, I could feel the belt attached to the headboard loosening. He let my wrists go, but he spun my body beneath his so that I was flat on my stomach, facedown on the bed.

"Bend your knees under you," he commanded.

I shivered as a pulse of desire went down my spine. I bent my knees.

He slid straight back inside of me, filling me up. My body clenched around his, and he grunted behind me.

I still couldn't move very much like this. I could only take what he gave me. A hand was between my shoulder blades to keep me down and help him keep his balance behind me.

He ravished me, plunging inside me again and again.

Grabbing my throat to pull my body down harder on his dick, he was so big and hard that it felt as if he was tearing my body into two. It was totally worth it. He shouted as he filled me with what felt like a liter of come. It spilled out onto my thighs and the sheets, getting everywhere.

His huge body collapsed on top of mine, with his dick still big inside of me. I had a little trouble breathing with so much weight on top of me, but I loved it. I loved feeling his sated body cage me.

After a few moments, he pulled his dick out of me, leaving a gaping, empty hole. He rolled to his side and spooned me. His arm came around my front to grip one of my breasts. He kissed my neck.

"That was spectacular, sweetheart," he told me. "You can do that with me anytime."

I caught his hand with my own and sucked his middle finger in reply.

I could feel him getting hard again behind me.

This time, it wasn't hard, fast, and untamed. It was slow and sweet. We stayed like that, in the spooning position. He brought my upper leg on top of his, and he slid his cock into my slick hole. I was still covered from his juices and mine from the first time.

His hand went to touch my clit. Every time that he pushed into me, he thrust me harder into his hand. He controlled my body with a slow rhythm.

I orgasmed quickly.

This time, he came over the edge with me. He shouted his pleasure as he released his hot seed inside of my body.

We lay there, on our sides, just catching our breaths.

Going to Canada

Naelle

"Where are we going now?"

While I loved the idea of staying on his boat, I knew that my dad could find us.

"We're going to Canada. We'll get a plane from there."

I held his close, smelling his wonderful scent. I could barely believe that we were back together.

I felt safe, warm, and happy. I touched my stomach. Our baby was in there.

My eyelids drooped.

"You're tired. Go to sleep."

"Okay," I said sleepily, yawning.

He kissed me. I fell asleep in his arms, felling the gentle motion of the boat as we moved towards the Canada.

* * *

I woke up to hear Emilio swearing in Spanish. He was pacing back and forth next to the bed, a phone in his hand. He seemed like a lion trapped in a cage.

I felt sorry for whomever he was talking to.

Finally, he hit the end call button.

"What's wrong?" I asked.

"They think that Alejandro is dead."

"What?"

I sat up on the bed, clutching the sheet to my chest. I felt very naked all of a sudden.

"He disappeared. The hotel staff took him to the hospital when he was having respiratory distress...it was inevitable for him to have a little trouble. He probably overdosed. He disappeared from his hospital bed."

"He could be fine," I soothed. "He might have just wandered off. Maybe he didn't like being in the hospital."

"Naelle," Emilio said very

quietly, "there was a lot of blood on his bed."

I felt the blood drain from my face.

"A lot of blood?"

"They think that he's dead and the Omegas stole his body."

"Oh, Emilio," I said, holding my arms out for a hug.

He sat on the edge of the bed. He put his head on my shoulder. I stroked his back and made soothing noises.

He wasn't crying, but I had the feeling that if things were slightly different, he would be.

"I should've been there," he said, his voice raspy and low from unshed tears.

"You were in America getting me back." I kissed his hair. "You can't do anything now. Wait until we get back to Ecuador, okay?"

I could feel the tension in his body.

"I hate being helpless and not knowing whether Alejandro is alive or not," he confessed.

I stroked his back a little more. I didn't have anything to say.

I sat in that bed, holding him for a little while.

Then he pulled away from me. When he turned to me, I saw a calm mask.

"We'll be fine as soon as we get

to the Canada. Our first stop in Ecuador will be to pick up Sofia."

"Who's that?"

"My niece."

Then I remembered that Alejandro had a daughter.

"Didn't he say that a nanny was taking care of her?"

"I'd feel more comfortable keeping her with me. They already took her father. Why do you think that they'd stop at Alejandro?"

"They wouldn't hurt a baby," I protested.

He twisted and gave me a look.

"I wouldn't stop. In the past, I haven't."

I felt my blood run cold.

"If you cross me, your family won't be safe. They're just repaying it in kind. The Omegas have hit me where it hurts the most. I shouldn't have cut Alejandro off from our own supply of cocaine. All of this is my fault."

"You couldn't know that he'd end up dead when you tried to clean him up. It's not your fault. You're not psychic."

"My family. My responsibility."

He walked out of the room. I had the sense that he'd cloaked himself in his drug lord persona.

I crawled out of bed. There was a small bathroom where I cleaned up before getting redressed in my clothing.

I went back and sat on the bed. I wasn't sure what was going to happen. I knew that I made the right choice, but everything was happening at once. I'd only met Alejandro once, but now we were going to go to their estate to pick up his daughter to protect her from a drug war. What a strange experience.

If I'd known about this when I'd decided to run to Ecuador after my horrible engagement party, I didn't know if I would've chosen this path.

But Emilio was worth everything that was going on right

now. I'd stick by him.

Halifax

Naelle

I lost track of time on the boat. Days passed, and I knew that my father hadn't found us. He probably was keeping an eye out, but he must know that I'd left of my own free will.

I spent my days hanging out on deck, trying not be in the way. Emilio was extremely grim throughout the journey. I knew that he still felt guilty. Finally, I saw land through the window.

"Here we are," Emilio said, putting an arm around me. "We'll fly down to the Bahamas, refuel, and go to Ecuador. I made a mistake when we went through Miami the first time. I won't make the mistake of refueling in the United States again."

"Okay."

As soon as we got out of the boat, there was a car waiting to take us to the airport. I'd never been to Nova Scotia before, but I wouldn't spend much time there.

It didn't take long for us to get to the airport. There was a different jet waiting for us there.

"Where's your jet?"

"Your father can trace it. I borrowed a jet from a friend,"

Emilio explained.

I didn't want to delve too deeply into it, but it was crazy that I was engaged to a man who could borrow a private jet at the drop of a hat.

Well, at least my baby would be born with a silver spoon in his mouth.

We got into the plane, went through all of the pre-flight stuff, and took off.

* * *

When I woke up, we must have already refueled in the Bahamas, because we were over the Caribbean. When I looked out my window, I could see tiny islands far below us.

Emilio had his laptop open. He was working.

I unbuckled my seatbelt and went over to him.

"Kiss, please."

He gave me a half grin and a quick kiss.

"How long will it be before we arrive in Ecuador?"

He looked at his watch.

"Not too long," he said. "I'm trying to find out what happened to Alejandro. The quantity of blood in the hospital would indicate that they killed him there and then took his dead body."

He looked so tired that it made

my heart ache.

"Is there anything I can do?"

"Just being with me helps. Knowing that you and the baby are safe means everything to me."

He grabbed my hand and kissed the back.

"I've been thinking about it...I've already sent most of my security guards to the family estate. We'll be able to keep everyone safe there. It's not like Quito. It's somewhat isolated, so it'll be better. We have our own private airstrip, as well."

"Okay."

"We're going to head straight there. You'll get to meet Sofia. I know that she'll like you."

I was good with kids, so I wasn't too worried.

After I kissed his soft hair, I left him to his work and went back to my seat. I fell asleep.

Estate

Naelle

I woke up when we landed on Emilio's estate. Out of the window, all I could see was green.

"We're here," he announced.

The pilots helped the plane come to a smooth stop. Emilio came over as I was unbuckling my seatbelt.

The two of us went out the doors.

"What about our luggage?"

"Someone will bring it later. My top priority is to keep you safe."

There was a small golf cart

waiting right there.

I knew that Emilio was a little more relaxed now that we were on his own land. He helped me into the cart before getting in himself. Our golf cart driver was wearing some sort of gray security uniform, and I could see a couple more guys with the same gray uniform scattered around the estate. It was as safe as Emilio could make it.

We went straight to the house, which was completely lit up. If I didn't already know that Emilio was very wealthy, the house would've convinced me. It looked like the kind of house that was featured in a magazine.

The golf cart came to a stop right in front of the house. Emilio thanked the driver before pulling me up the steps and into the house.

"Sofia!" he bellowed. "Where's Sofia?"

"Miyo?" I heard a little voice call.

Through the slats of the balcony on the second floor, I could see a little girl. She didn't look too steady on her feet. I was worried about her falling.

I ran up the stairs faster than Emilio.

"Hey there, sweetie." I reached for her, but she just backed away.

My heart was beating fast — I didn't know if it was from my sprint up the stairs or from how close she was to the edge of the balcony.

"Miyo!" she said with a little more urgency.

"It's okay, I'm here," Emilio said, scooping her into his arms.

The three of us walked into what must have been her nursery. It was as if the Easter Bunny had set off a pastel bomb in there. Everything was pastel pink.

"It's past somebody's bedtime," Emilio said, looking at his watch.

She obediently closed her eyes, her little arms around Emilio's neck. He sat in the corner in a rocking chair, gently patting her back.

Father's Raid

Naelle

Emilio had just gotten Sofia to fall asleep when the nursery door opened with a bang. It crashed into the wall.

"Where's Naelle?" my father shouted.

"Shh," I told him. "You'll scare the baby."

With a wail, the baby started to freak out.

Emilio jiggled the baby, trying to make her stop crying. It seemed as if she wanted to go for the Guinness World Record for loudest screams.

I went to the door and saw men with guns and full gear in the hallway, as if this were some sort of raid.

"I think that there's been a misunderstanding," I apologized.

Two of the guys were stoic and must've been fathers or something, because they were completely fine with hearing a baby scream bloody murder.

The youngest team member looked like he wanted to cover his ears.

"I think that you won't be needed today."

My dad was behind me, still in

the doorway and staring at Emilio with Alejandro's daughter.

"Dismissed," he told the guys.

They looked at each other for a moment before hightailing it out of there. They must've sensed that it was family drama.

When they were gone, my father shook his head and covered his eyes with his hand.

"Good Lord," he said. "What a mess." He took his hand away from his eyes and looked straight at me.

"You're happy here? You weren't kidnapped? You're here of your own free will?"

"Yes...to everything."

He took a look at the baby in

Emilio's arms, who had finally stopped crying and was staring at my dad with big eyes.

"Baby," I cooed, "do you want to meet my daddy, huh?"

I picked her up and kissed her little forehead.

I put her in my dad's arms. Her big eyes stared into his.

And then she smiled.

In that moment, I saw all of his defenses melt away.

"Hey there, pumpkin." He smiled at her.

"That's my name," I mock-protested.

The three of us laughed, which made Sofia let out a little gurgle.

"I think she likes you," I said as I watched her little hand pat his cheek.

"I think I like her," my dad said, jiggling her a little in his arms. He put his nose right in her little bit of fine baby hair.

"She's ours unless Alejandro shows up," I said. "She's your adoptive granddaughter."

"Granddaughter, huh?"

"And she's going to be joined by a grandson." I touched my stomach.

"You're having a baby?"

"Yup."

A strange smile came to his face — it sat there strangely, as if he weren't sure that he should be smiling.

"I'll look forward to meeting him," he said finally.

I went to look at Emilio, love in my eyes. He met my eyes. I saw a whole lot of love reflected back at me.

Epilogue

Naelle

MORE THAN TWO YEARS LATER

"Ernesto, stop that!"

My little troublemaker just giggled and took another chunk of his birthday cake. When he jammed it into his mouth, he got sweet frosting all over his chubby cheeks.

"We're supposed to save that for your second birthday party, Ernesto!" My parents were coming. My dad had retired as soon as I married Emilio, though only my mom came to my wedding. It had taken a while for my dad to really warm up to Emilio, but Ernesto had definitely helped. Emilio leaving the drug business had helped, too; he didn't want any of his family members being killed by the Omegas. Now, we were one of the major exporters of quinoa to the United States; it was grown in the same fields by the same farmers, and it helped that it was aboveboard and a little easier to transport and distribute. We didn't have to worry about the government flying crop-duster planes with chemicals that would ruin the crop. We'd cleaned the house from top to bottom to prepare for them, but Ernesto had ruined his birthday cake before the party even started.

Emilio walked into the kitchen carrying Sofia, who looked precious in her sparkly pink dress. I had put her hair in a French braid that morning. It was already falling apart, but she was just cute as ever. She may have been my niece, but we treated her like our own daughter. Despite Emilio's efforts to find him, Alejandro hadn't shown up, and he was most likely dead. Sofia was our little ray of sunshine, our precious angel who looked more like Alejandro every day.

He saw the destroyed cake and the red-handed cake thief.

"Don't worry, cari," he told me. "We'll get another cake."

I just shook my head as he put his free arm around me. I leaned into his strong body.

"Honestly — if this is what Ernesto is like now, I can't imagine what he'll be like as a teenager."

"We'll handle it." He kissed my cheek.

"Together, we can do anything."

This is a work of fiction